INFLUENCERS AND ORDINARIES

VIOLA TEMPEST

Viola Tempest Publishing

Influencers and Ordinaries
© Copyright 2022 Viola Tempest

Cover Design by Wanderlust Ink & Tome
Website: https://wanderlustinktome.com

Contents

Chapter 1

April, 2019

On my way home from work, I have no choice but to walk past the Wall. It's a route I can't get around, one I am used to, one I have been walking all my life. That doesn't make it any less hard to deal with.

In fact, now, it's even worse. Now that it's Abigail and Ariel in the top ten.

She got the news last night, like all the other wannabe Influencers, all the hopefuls who'd been chosen for the annual tournament. The competition — which was too nice a word to describe what the event truly was — had been enacted in the year 2049, over three decades before I was even born. That means, since that day sixty years ago, there have been almost six hundred deaths. Six hundred deaths you can link back to nothing important, nothing except my two least favorite words: social media.

Can you tell I'm kind of in a bad mood today?

Anyway. The Wall.

It sits in the middle of New California, not far from

where Hollywood once was back in the olden days before movies and television stopped production. Back then, this town had been bustling. Now, it's a ghost town. Well, this whole *nation's* a ghost town. But that's another story for another time.

The Wall is long, and I mean *long*. Think of it like those giant bodies of water that span entire states, like Lake Michigan. Except, this Wall spans entire *continents*. Well, the developed ones anyway, the ones with Internet capability. Which is just about everywhere.

They started building it back in 2030, right around the time that the CEO of HXT, the biggest social media platform on the planet, became even more influential than the President. It took nearly two decades to build. Why? Because Influencers and Ordinaries are *everywhere*, not just here in the United States.

The Wall had to be vast enough to separate us, no matter where on the planet we lived. Which means that the Wall on my route to work is the same Wall that businessmen in London and children in India pass by. The entire world is divided, factionalized by that one wall, the wall no one but *them* can get past.

I'm just gonna tell you right now — I'm an outlier. Ever since I was little, I never understood why so many people were obsessed with social media. Mind you, back then, I hadn't reached the point of *hatred* yet, just disinterest. I never understood the appeal of having a million eyes watching you every second of the day, never comprehended how so many people could lose their entire lives in a rectangular device.

Although, with all the commercials they play nowadays, it's easy to see why my little sister got sucked in. They — meaning the CEO of HXT and everyone doing her biddings — do a good job of drawing you into their world by making you feel like your world is worthless. Of course, it's only dangling a carrot in front of a horse. No one ever gets over the Wall. The tournament that starts today kills more people than it fulfills dreams.

I hate social media, hate the Influencers, hate everything the Wall and the exclusive world beyond represents. But as I walk past the border that April evening, the sun going down with a splash of pink-orange and vivid violet on the horizon, I'm wishing Ariel wins.

Watch me tonight! That's what Ariel had said, so cheerily (already *talking* like the Influencers before she even won), that morning when she called me from the location. Where the location is located, I have no idea. It's one of the many things that HXT and its CEO get away with just not telling anyone.

Ariel had said it was a ghost town like ours, but a *real* one, one in some rural place where there were only farmland and old, abandoned buildings. Perfect place for a bunch of people to start murdering each other over likes, followers, and audience votes.

Ridiculous. Ridiculous, but I turn the program on, anyway. Because Ariel asked me to. And there's not much I won't do for Ariel.

For a moment, before the live streaming starts, I sit in my dimly-lit living room and watch the commercials flash across my phone. A familiar face, belonging to Loren Harper, the most popular Influencer in the world, lights up the screen with her perfect blonde hair, white teeth, and slim body. She is the It Girl, the one everyone aspires to be, the one my own little sister has posters of in her bedroom. No matter where you go, what you watch, you can never get away from Loren's flawless, perpetually happy face.

Right then, she's advertising some new cosmetic that promises to "make you look like your favorite Influencer!"

The commercial shows Loren smilingly dabbing at her face with a foundation-soaked sponge, everything about her face so perfect that it almost looks *unreal,* like a plastic doll's face.

Her final punch line before the screen fades is this: *"Can't get over the Wall? No problem! Now, you can look like me, and share a little bit of Influencer happiness!"*

I sigh and shake my head. There's no telling how many thirteen-year-olds she just sent into a deep depression with that twenty-second commercial. It's no wonder this whole town is in such darkness, such poverty.

I feel myself growing annoyed, wanting to switch my device off. Thankfully, the streaming starts at that exact second, and my nervous anticipation at seeing my sister on the screen overtakes everything else. I sit forward on the couch, anxiously gripping my phone.

And then she appears. They all do, one by one. The start of the show reminds me of ancient footage of that century-old show, The Mickey Mouse Club, where all the cast members introduce themselves with just a quick, snappy exclamation of their name. The Tournament's logo appears (with *Sponsored by HXT* in fine print at the bottom), and then all ten of the contestants flash across the screen in peppy, heavily-produced succession.

"Bryn!" announces a fifteen-year-old boy with glossy, perfectly arranged blonde hair and an ultra-white smile. His country's flag appears beneath his face — it's the Wales flag.

"Jeena!" cries a twenty-one-year-old girl with a faint accent from South Korea.

"Mason!"

"Aaron!"

"Kristy!"

"Jorge!"

"Shreya!"

"Ava!"

"Chase!"

Back-to-back, all nine of them appear for a two-second instant to declare their name and show their country. Not that the whole world doesn't already know everything there is to know about them. They're the people with the most followers in the Ordinary World. They're as close to Influencer status as you can get without actually going over the Wall.

At last, my sister is shown. It took her five grueling years, since she was twelve years old, to get to the point where she was chosen for the top ten Ordinary profiles. I watched her cry, stay up late, waste money, and all but kill herself just to gain Internet attention. But you can't tell it when she appears on the screen. She looks like the others, like a girl who's had an easy life. You can't tell that, up until now, she lived with her brother on the edge of poverty because her parents died from a disease that couldn't be cured, now that all the doctors live on the other side of the Wall.

You can't tell that I raised her on a meager, assemblyman's salary, barely feeding her from the wages I make assembling selfie sticks and ring lights all day. All you see is a face radiating with makeup and beauty, her brown eyes warm and sparkling, her dark hair silky and long, her crop top and shorts showing off a thin body she put through way too many dangerous diets to achieve.

And then she cries her name, "Ariel!" And it takes everything I have in me to keep from throwing my phone across the room. I'm happy to see her, but no amount of joy can take away from the pain at knowing what's coming for her. She's gorgeous, the prettiest one of the ten, in my opinion, but she's low on the totem pole in terms of followers. She *barely* made it into the top ten. I worry she'll be one of the first ones killed, and at the same time, I worry she'll end up the winner. Either way, the system will destroy my little sister.

Her spotlight ends quickly, and then the camera pans to show all ten of the contestants lined up on an empty street in front of a giant skyscraper that looked like it was once a big city mall. But Ariel was right — the whole place is a ghost town now. It's gray, and dark, and you can practically see tumbleweeds rolling past. But the contestants, with their glittery faces and bright clothes, add color to the screen. They stand out, each of them with perfect smiles fixed in place.

The camera shifts to a TV hostess standing on the edge of the group, a little apart from the hopefuls. Like them, she is a pristinely-arranged woman, clearly someone from the other side of the Wall, but not quite Influencer status. She's in her late forties, and the evidence of many plastic surgeries in the bizarre stiffness of her cheeks and lips.

She announces, "Welcome to the sixtieth annual Influencer Tournament!" and then launches into the same speech they give every year, where they talk about how nice and benevolent the CEO of HXT was to invent the tournament. They think she did this wonderful thing by allowing nine people to be murdered every year.

Their reasoning? Apparently, she had saved the Ordinaries from their intense depression by allowing hardworking hopefuls the chance to become an Influencer, which is everyone in their right mind's greatest aspiration.

I don't buy any of it. I don't buy *anything* that woman tries to sell us, especially since she herself is so secretive. No one's ever seen her face. No one even knows her name. She's the mastermind behind the social system geared toward total transparency, toward everyone knowing everyone. Yet, she's the biggest enigma of all.

Once the speech is over, the cameraperson takes a moment to go down the line of contestants, highlighting each of them. Their personal details, such as name, age, and country, are briefly touched on. But most of the attention is placed on how many followers their social profile has, how many likes and comments each of their posts brings in, how *buzzworthy* they are.

By their standards, the most important member of the group is Bryn, the boy from Wales. I can understand why. He has the face a teenage girl would go wild over. But I can't help but wonder how much of it is real, and how much of it is money spent to make it that way.

The second most important contestant is Shreya, the exotic beauty from New Delhi. She's only twelve, but dresses like somebody twice her age. That's nothing abnormal, though. They don't sell modest clothes in the shops. I'm not even sure they make them anymore. If they did, nobody would buy them, because they all want to look like their skin-exposed idols.

At the end of the group, my sister is announced as seventeen-year-old Ariel from the outskirts of New California. But that isn't important. The hostess glosses right over that. Instead, her follower count is lingered on. She has a whopping one hundred thousand, which seems like a big number to me, but makes the others standing next to her cringe and look at her sideways, almost like they're already making plans to kill her first. Get rid of the weaker ones before anyone else.

The hostess puts Ariel down because of this number, too. She says, though with a perky smile, "That's quite a low number! To my knowledge, you almost didn't make the cut for the tournament. Am I right, Ariel?"

"That's right." My sister smiles glitteringly.

She looks so young, so vulnerable. I hate to imagine what will happen in the days to come.

"Well, we're glad you managed to beat the odds! You never know, maybe this year will be the year of the underdog!"

I hope so. And yet, I don't.

Introductions are over now, so the hostess goes into the competition rules. These, like the speech, have never been changed since 2049. You would think that after nearly six hundred deaths, someone would think to modify the rules so violence wasn't allowed. But they don't, because it's great for ratings.

The rules are simple: the competition lasts a week. The goal? To have the highest social numbers out of everyone by the end of the week — which encompasses follower count, number of comments, and number of likes. And this isn't just the social profiles on HXT — less popular social media platforms are included, like TenSec, the platform on which people get famous just for uploading videos as short as ten seconds, and Rankface, which is nothing but a giant poll system, where people upload pictures of themselves, and viewers rank them based on their beauty.

In order to climb up the social ladder during the tournament, contestants will be required to post daily, on all three platforms, at all times of the day. Why all times of the day? Because if one girl is posting all night, and another girl chooses to actually go to bed, the one who sleeps will probably lose about a billion followers overnight to the one who forgoes essential bodily needs. Then again, that all-night girl will probably end up getting wiped out at some point.

Because that's where the rules get tricky. Technically,

the goal is to have the highest numbers. But the goal is also to be the last one standing at the end of the week. So technically, a profile with low numbers could end up winning, *if* they're cunning, careful, and violent enough.

Nothing is fair, and anything goes. The contestants not only have to step on their fellow contestants to gain social prowess, but they also have to survive. They have to make sure their basic human needs are supplied. So far, it looks like they'll be staying in that abandoned mall. It will probably come stocked with food. But again, the anything goes thing. Someone could easily steal their own supply of food, then destroy all the rest in hopes of starving the other contestants, and that would be totally legal and fair. There's no telling what these attention-starved people will do.

My stomach lurches when the countdown kicks off. Sixty seconds until the group is shoved into the building, and the hostess locks the doors, locks them in with each other.

I pray Ariel is resourceful. I pray she knows how to take care of herself. And I wish, wish with all the frustration inside me, that I had taught her something about self-defense. But all she grew up knowing was the device that never left her hand. All I'd done for her was provide food for her belly, and keep the bills paid for our parents' home so she would have a roof over her head. She'd practically raised herself.

I'm almost overwhelmed with a sense of failure, but I can't let myself go down that road. It's too late now.

The countdown hits zero.

The hostess announces in a crisp, perky voice, "Let the tournament begin!"

And then the chaos ensues.

Chapter 2

It's rare for children not to be gifted smartphones immediately after they're born. It's as much a tradition as cutting the umbilical cord or buying diapers. That's another one of the ways HXT's CEO is seen as a benevolent woman. She bought out major cell phone companies decades ago, and has been giving the devices away for free ever since.

In history textbooks, school kids learn about a time in the early twenty-first century, when phones used to be *expensive.* They shudder, and at the same time frown, because such a notion is incomprehensible. Phones cost nothing to manufacture now, and social media platforms want people to have phones as early as possible so they can continue powering their empire and the entire world that occurs on the other side of the Wall.

A lot of times, I think about the old days and lament about the century I was raised in. It must have been strange back then, when babies were given toys instead of flashing screens. Weird, but peaceful. I envy the twenty-first century children as my own eyes stay glued to my phone, watching the tournament kick off in full swing.

There are cameras placed in nearly every inch of that mall, providing high-definition footage of everything the contestants are doing at a given time. When they first run in, they immediately split up. The group breaks as individuals flee in opposite directions. It's always like this at the start. People make sure their needs are taken care of as soon as competition begins. Then, as the days go on, and more and more people are... *eliminated*, that's when alliances start being formed.

But for now, it's every man and woman for themselves.

Some of them already have their smartphone in hand; they're the ones rushing around in a hunt for perfect lighting, eager to get their first post up.

Others have fled straight for the makeup counters to stock up on beauty products before someone cruel decides to take them all for his or herself.

My eyes blow up as the camera zeroes in on a couple of girls in the cosmetics section. Jeena, the girl from South Korea, and Kristy, the one hailing from up north in New Illinois. They've both got their eye on the same product: a bottle of foundation in a very specific color. It's the only bottle left. The brand is a world-renowned one, also owned by HXT's CEO. Is there anything that bitch *doesn't* own?

After a second, it becomes clear why the tournament's production team decided to focus on this moment. They always do this when a fight is about to break out.

I can see it, too. Already, these two girls hate each other. For a moment, they just stand there, glares passing between them. Kristy's stare looks more cunning — right off the bat, I can tell that she's the type who would smile to your face while she holds a knife behind her back. Jeena's expression is more transparent, blatantly murderous. It's as if you can clearly see all the ways she wants to kill Kristy in her black-mirror eyes.

I hold my breath.

Then one of the girls — Kristy — pounces, snatching up the last bottle of foundation with a blurred movement that Jeena barely catches. But when she *does* notice what her opponent just did, all hell breaks loose.

Jeena's eyes flash toward Kristy — and in that one instance, the camera does a great job of capturing the obvious *snap* that has just occurred inside her. Somehow, I know what she's going to do before she does it. She lashes out, snatching up Kristy's arm and yanking her backwards just as she starts to run. Not keen on watching — or hearing — this, I hastily press my finger to the volume button, silencing my phone. I squeeze my eyes shut and count to ten.

When I open them again and turn the volume back up, there's blood all over the cosmetics department floor. The bright red color oozing all over the tiles is shown in its entirety. None of the gory details are censored for TV, not even the corpse. She is spotlighted for a good half minute — and then her glittery headshot appears on the screen. A caption beneath reads: KRISTEN MEYERS, FIRST ONE OUT. A blaring red X flashes across her face, signifying her demise and official exit from the tournament.

Then everything disappears: the X, the picture, the dead body. Done with her, the camera shifts its focus to other areas of the mall, and the competition continues.

———

No one else dies for the rest of the day, which is a relief. Most of the other contestants just stay away from one another. They hole themselves up in isolated corners (provided the lighting is good) and keep busy smiling and posing for their phone cameras, making videos, and raking in the likes and comments. I don't watch the whole time, but keep the streaming on in the background while I make dinner.

On my salary, I can't afford much food. Just a few loaves of bread, a sack of rice, and a pack of frozen fake meat that's meant to last a good six months. It's been decades since there have been any real farms. All the food we eat now is designed in laboratories.

Like with many of the theories about life over the Wall being significantly better, there are rumors that *their* world has much lush agriculture, producing tons and tons of fresh produce for the Influencers. Of course, there are also a lot of ridiculous rumors, like giant pools of water the Influencers bathe in *for fun.*

After I eat my sparse meal, which tastes, frankly, like textured cardboard, I shed my clothes and step into the steamer box. As the fine mists come on, technologically configured to spray for five minutes, washing me of the dirt and toxins I accumulated in the factory, I think about other stories I've heard about life over the Wall. Stories about bars of soap that foam up into sweet-smelling suds. It's something they used to have a century ago. Could the Influencers really possess such a luxury?

They sure make it seem like it. Everything, every commercial, every picture, every article, makes their world seem like paradise on Earth. And the people who rule social media further amplify that notion. They rave on and on about their perfect life, not just talking about it alone, but showing it off in the form of flawlessly-snapped photographs and videos. It's no wonder why every year, people are so eager to fight to the death for even a meager chance at going over the Wall.

After my shower, I settle in for the night, watching as things calm down in the tournament. The camera pans to different parts of the mall, showing the contestants preparing for the night. Some of them are looking for a place to lay their head and sleep. Others are setting up their cameras to film a perfect nightly routine video.

My sister is one of the few focused on shelter. I feel a surge of pride as I watch her march up the aisles, searching for a safe place to sleep. She's smart. She's resourceful. Just as I'd hoped.

A lot of people are idiots. They go down to the basement where all the home goods are and pick out one of the plush king-sized beds that stands out in the open, exposed for any and every one to see. Ariel is smarter. She visits the bedding section briefly, just to collect a couple blankets and some feather pillows to take back upstairs to the clothing department.

No one is on this floor; no one sees her. She traps herself in one of the fitting rooms and lays out her bedding, turning it into a makeshift hotel room. Here, she'll be safe for the night. I guarantee the people who chose to camp out in the beds will be dead by morning.

But I feel a lot better now. My nerves are more at ease. I know now that, at least for tonight, my little sister is going to be okay.

Chapter 3

I had social media once. I know, hard to believe, right? Well, it didn't last very long, trust me.

I grew up like a lot of guys, watching the male Influencers entice and snatch the attention of all the girls in the world. After failing to get the attention of a classmate I had the biggest crush on when she declared me, "so much uglier than Hansel Bridgestone," the pretty boy who was one of the biggest Influencers at the time, I strived to become an Influencer myself.

I wasted three years of my life doing odd jobs, just to pay for expensive hair salon sessions, cosmetics, and the highest-grade selfie sticks and ring lights on the market. I nearly got expelled from school twice, all because I was too busy staying up late to post picture after picture and video after video in my quest to gain a following. I was always too exhausted to even do homework, let alone go to school. Finally, I had to face up to the fact that I'd wasted nearly all of high school, and now, had no chance of becoming anything other than a menial worker. Still, at least I had a way to support Ariel. Things could be worse.

They could also be so much better.

The winner of the tournament don't just win popularity, gazillions of followers, and accolade. They also get a check for a million dollars, a brand-new home over the Wall that comes equipped with two or three servants, fridge and pantry stocked with the best food, and *eternal glory*. Or, at least, that's how Loren Harper had described it when she'd given her official tournament endorsement a month ago.

All the up-high Influencers do. I'm not sure how much of it is true, and how much of those words are empty, things they're simply paid to say. But I do know that I don't want my sister to live in poverty anymore. And if she could just... *stay alive* long enough...

But my hope in that fantasy quickly deteriorates as the tournament progresses.

In just four days, already more than half of the competition has been wiped out. They've all been killed in brutal ways, each death more disturbing than the last. But the deaths aren't important to the audience and the CEO of HXT — only the rankings are. Up until now, the murdered contestants have been the ones with the lowest numbers: Mason, Chase, Ava, Jorge, and Aaron. But now is when the competition gets interesting — or terrifying, however you want to look at it. Because now, the battle is between the four topmost wannabes on the Influencer totem pole. Jeena, who reigns supreme not only because of her numbers, but also because she's been the one doing most of the killings. She's coldhearted and has an eerie glint in her eyes. I've gotten to where I flinch every time it's her turn to flash across the screen.

The others are Shreya, Bryn, and Ariel. Yup. Somehow, my little sister makes it into the top four.

On Friday morning, the countdown begins. Only two days left. Two days until a victor is crowned. Per the tradition, all activity is halted for a half hour as the stiff-faced hostess from before is brought in to do live interviews with the remaining contestants. I get up early to watch this before work.

At ten till six, my device lights up in my hand as the screen changes from mall atmosphere to dead-street scenery. Like déjà vu, the camera shows the hostess standing out on the sidewalk in front of the mall, just like she did four days ago when the competition started.

But now, instead of ten contestants facing her, there are only four. Jeena is first in the line. My sister is at the end of it. Again.

"Welcome, viewers of the world!" the hostess announces, smile fixed in place. "It's that time again! We have reached the last half of the competition, and now, it's time for our midpoint interview session. Let's start with Jeena, the crowd favorite hailing from South Korea."

Jeena lifts her chin as a proud smirk spreads across her face. I watch her with awe in my gaze. She's the only contestant who has yet to *sleep*. For four straight days, she's done nothing but dress up in a gazillion outfits for pictures, post videos of herself, and slink around like a panther and murder anyone who isn't sharp enough to notice her coming.

No sleep for four days. Yet, you'd never be able to tell if you just saw her now, without having seen any of the live-streamed footage of the past few days. She is as bright and chipper as ever, her cheeks flushed and dewy, makeup done with flawless precision, hair luscious and positioned just right, outfit the right combination of cute and intimidating.

I'm wondering how she hasn't collapsed yet, when the hostess launches into her interview.

"Jeena, in terms of numbers, you remain our most popular contestant. Since the competition started on Monday, you have posted two hundred times and racked in an impressive three million new followers, eight hundred thousand comments, and four million likes."

Jeena smiles and nods. There goes that creepy glint again. It appears every now and then. When she's looking at herself in the mirror, admiring her reflection. When she's killing someone. And now, when she's wallowing in pride from all the compliments thrown her way. I hope and pray she isn't the winner.

"But Jeena, it isn't just the numbers you've excelled at," the hostess continues. "You have also gained fame from your interactions with the other contestants. Let's take a look at some of your finest moments."

At this, the scene changes to a video montage. As if they weren't hard enough to watch the first time, a replay of every murder Jeena has committed flashes across the screen again. I'm astonished to see that Jeena killed five times — which means, she's been the only one to kill so far. As each of her crimes is played back for the audience to relish in again, I shake my head in disbelief.

I've grown up watching the tournament, grown up seeing many contestants die at the hands of someone a little bit extra violent. But Jeena is the worst by far. My blood runs cold as I realize something: she'll be impossible to beat. She *wants* it too much. The only way she'll lose is if someone kills her. But she's too busy killing everyone else before they can even *try*. My sister Ariel doesn't stand a chance.

Finally, the playback montage ends, and when the

camera cuts back to the live version of Jeena, she's… *laughing.*

The hostess chuckles nervously. "You seem quite proud of what we've just seen. Do you have any comment on your performance thus far?"

Jeena shrugs, still grinning. "All I can say is… I *will* be the next Influencer."

She leaves it at that, simple. But her eyes and devious smirk convey far more than her words could. I'm relieved when the focus moves onto the next contestant.

After Bryn and Shreya give their two cents about how the competition has gone so far, the camera pans to Ariel. At this point, it's time for me to get ready for work. I slide out of bed, but keep my eyes glued to the screen as I hobble to the kitchen for my morning gruel.

"Ariel, my dear!" the hostess exclaims, cheerily, while the camera latches onto my sister's nervous smile. "You sure have caused quite a ruckus this season!"

She has? I don't know — I don't keep up with what people talk about online. Has Ariel been doing better than I thought?

With an endearing giggle, Ariel shrugs her shoulders and bites her lip while a true blush, one not achieved by pigmented cosmetics, blooms in her cheeks. I notice something, watching this brief display of her nerves. She's the only one of the four who actually seems *human.* Though she sports the same flawless makeup, trendy outfit, and silky hair as the others, she is set apart. Not in looks, in demeanor. The others are like dolls. Shreya and Bryn are Barbie and Ken, while Jeena is Chucky. But Ariel seems like a real person. Is that why she's causing a ruckus?

I shut my brain up so I can focus on the next words out of the hostess' mouth.

"I must admit, Ariel. When you first came in, I thought you would be the first one out. Not that you're not gorgeous, of course. It's your *stats*, you see. Your numbers have consistently been the lowest in the competition. However, for the first time since this tournament has started, the underdog contestant has caused the most widespread uproar! Seventy percent of the daily comments on our live streaming pertain to you, Ariel. People *love* you! What do you think is the reason for this?"

Ariel gives a sheepish grin, and for a moment, my heart swells, and a smile tugs on my lips because she looks five again. I used to tell her stories of the old days, things I'd gleaned from stumbling on ancient films and television shows online. When she was that young, I used to ask her stuff like, "Have you ever heard of this thing called a *boy band*?" and "Do you know about the great Amazon company?" And she'd always get that guilty little grin and shake her head, almost as if she were embarrassed to say no. That was the smile she displayed now, a smile twelve years older, but still the same, still just as adorable.

"I'm not sure," she answers honestly.

The camera briefly cuts to Jeena, showing the unimpressed grimace she's sending my sister's way. It makes me want to reach my hands inside the phone and wring her neck.

Thankfully, the screen changes back to the hostess.

"Well, I think *I* know!" she declares. "Let's take a look at Ariel's most talked-about moments from this week!"

Just like with Jeena, Bryn, and Shreya, my sister gets about a minute and a half of video montage time. And when her playback starts, I immediately realize the answer. I know why my sister is a crowd favorite. It's because she's *resourceful*.

The first scene they show is the same one that filled me with pride. The one where she cleverly built her camp in one of the fitting rooms in the mall. Then they show what she was *doing* eighty percent of the time, inside that fitting room. She was the only one of all ten contestants to actually *watch* the live stream. The thought seemed to cross no one else's minds — they all just used their phones for one purpose only: posting content.

Ariel posts too, and often. But she switches focus intermittently, too. The footage shows her watching the live stream, seeing where her opponents are at any given moment. Through this, she is able to creep out of her hiding spots and steal food from the empty food court when no one is around, grab clothes when the racks are deserted, and makeup when the cosmetic counter is vacant. She sees when murders take place and knows where to be to avoid her own death. She's smart because she doesn't have a one-track mind. Everyone else's main goal is numbers. Follower count, likes, comments. According to the footage, Ariel's main goal is *survival.*

The video montage finally ends, and the first thing the camera shows is the bewildered, ghost-white faces of the other contestants standing beside my sister. You can see it, the realization crashing down on them all at once. They're thinking: *Why didn't I think of that? Why didn't I check the live stream?*

But I realize something with a pang of horror.

Now that they know to watch the other contestants, now that they know the exact location of my sister's hiding place, now that they know *she's* the crowd favorite, she'll have a target on her back.

Chapter 4

On my way to work, I pass the Wall. Inevitable.

Normally, I walk on, increasing the speed of my gait so I can get away from that place. But now, something makes me pause. Something makes me risk being late for work to turn, lift my eyes, and stare at it.

The Wall is at least a hundred feet high and made of thick, strong materials. On the outside, it just looks like one strip of concrete. But I know from talking to one of the older workers at the factory, one whose father was one of the people to help build the massive fence, that there are actually multiple layers to the Wall. There is concrete, cement, *and* iron.

The Wall's height ensures that no one will be able to climb over. Its lack of a door or gate on our side ensures that no one will be able to just walk through. And its density ensures that no one will have the power to break it down. There is a rumor that there's a door on the Influencer side of the Wall. But nobody knows if that's true.

Once a year, when the tournament winner is picked,

they are not taken to the Influencer World through the Wall. Instead, a helicopter is flown in, and they are taken in that way.

It goes without saying that it's impossible for an ordinary person to just waltz into the Influencer World. The Wall does a good job of preventing that.

At work, people are already making bets. Instead of assembling the devices that turn ordinary people into wannabe Influencers, my coworkers sit outside of the factory and lay wagers on who they think will be the next one killed, and who they think will be the winner. They do this every year, and every year, I've declined to give my bet.

At this point, the others know me so well that they don't even ask me to join. I'm glad. Of all the years, this is the one I *especially* don't want to bet on.

But I hear their opinions as I stride past.

"I'm betting on Jeena. That girl is *ruthless*."

"Yeah, but Zachary's little sister is gaining numbers. She's definitely the crowd favorite."

"Won't matter if she gets killed."

I grit my teeth and quicken my gait, hurrying inside so I don't have to hear anymore. They're right about everything. Jeena *is* ruthless, and my little sister *is* the crowd favorite. They're also right when they say that numbers won't change anything — not if Ariel ends up dead. The real goal of the tournament has never been to have the highest numbers. The real goal is to be the last one standing.

When I clock in and head to the main assembly room, my eyes immediately go to the two giant screens leaning against the back wall. Yes, we have televisions in the factory. Normally, they're kept in a storage room, but every April, they're wheeled out so the workers can be up to date on tournament stuff.

One screen shows the live stream (the contestant named Bryn is currently on display; he's hiding in an out-of-order elevator). The other shows the twenty-four-hour news.

The headline on the news screen reads: *RIOTS CONTINUE — 500 DEATHS.*

I sigh, watching the gruesome footage that plays out. There are always social media-related deaths throughout the year, but it's worse during the tournament.

Trying to ignore the screens, I focus on my task. The daily quota is always one thousand selfie sticks and one thousand ring lights. I have a lot to do.

And normally, I would be working hard. On a typical day, I would just work like a mindless robot, barely even noticing the motions of my hands as they work. I would do my job like the rest of them, questioning nothing, indulging none of my own desires.

But today — what is it about today? — something makes me pause.

Something makes me actually look at what I'm doing… and *stop*.

I stare at all the parts that make up the selfie stick I'm supposed to be assembling and feel a wave of disgust barrel into me. Disgust at these silly sticks designed to hold up an even sillier device. Disgust at the devices themselves, which have ruled society for nearly a century now. Disgust at the man who owns them, the man who presides over social media, the man in charge of all the killings. Disgust at the *system.*

And disgust at myself, for being part of the system, for furthering it, for coming to work every day to make it stronger, to create even more opportunities for some depressed individual to pick up their device and start the long, hard, endless journey to becoming an "Influencer."

Influencer. It's a stupid term, I think. But it fits. The Influencers *influence.*

They influence people to believe that life over the Wall is a perfect fairytale, and that all of its inhabitants are sorrow-free happiness machines.

They influence people to spend billions of dollars a year on cosmetics, plastic surgery, and technology.

They influence people to give themselves up to be murdered every year in April when the tournament starts, on the pretense that they themselves will hold the coveted Influencer position one day.

They influence people to suffer through depression, poverty, and riots.

They influence friends to backstab friends, young children to go on dangerous diets, and parents to blow their paychecks on hordes of fake "followers" for their children, purchased at a hefty price.

They influence people to be okay with greed, murder, betrayal, rioting, starving, suicide — all in the name of rising to the top.

Influencers, alright.

"Hey. What's the matter, Zachary? Why aren't you working?"

The voice stops me in my tracks. Thank goodness. I almost went off the rails.

It's my supervisor, peering over my shoulder and wondering what has gripped me, what has caused me to display such abnormal behavior.

I just smile, mutter a dumb, generic excuse, and get back to work.

But I don't work as eagerly as I normally do. I don't lose myself in the job, abandoning my thoughts to nothingness.

I think *hard,* through every step of the process. All

about the problems in society, and the people in charge of creating them.

———

When I go home that night, I eat dinner in front of the screen. Thankfully, nothing happens that night. Nobody dies. The four contestants remain — Jeena, Bryn, Shreya, and Ariel. They alternate between posting to their social profiles and watching the live stream on their phones, checking up on the others and seeing what they're up to.

At this point, they all know where each other is. They can see clearly, at any given moment, each other's whereabouts. They know where each of them have set up camp for the night. They know, and they watch, but nobody makes the first move. Tensions mount to a height I don't think has ever existed, in *any* tournament. This year will be the one to make history, in more ways than one. I can feel it.

But pretty soon, I am yawning, my hands aching from hours of putting useless devices together. The live stream is quiet, and so is the warm house. So, I put my phone away, strip my clothes off, and crawl into bed for the night.

Chapter 5

Saturday morning, I wake to a barrage of news.

So much has happened in the middle of the night, so much has changed while I was asleep in sheets and oblivion.

There are only two contestants now. Two of them, Bryn and Shreya, were killed in cold blood. By Jeena. She is, of course, one of the two still remaining.

My sister, Ariel, is the other.

For a good five minutes after I find out, I run around the house in a blaze of joy, reverting to my childhood self when things were simpler, and I was unaware of the hideousness of this world. I smile and laugh and punch the air in my elation, knowing that Ariel is just one step closer, *just one step closer,* to taking this whole thing home, to winning it all, and beginning her life over the Wall.

Then I come back to Earth. I come back to the live stream and the rest of the news report waiting for me.

That's when the joy seeps out of me.

Because I see something horrific: Ariel may be alive, but she *was* attacked. Jeena *did* try to kill her. The footage flashes in violent clarity on my screen. First, the murders of Bryn and Shreya are shown. In the middle of the night, fatigue overtook both of them. They fell asleep, fell into their death sentence. The moment they stopped watching their screens, stopped observing the others' activity, Jeena (who *never* stopped observing the others, who never even *slept*) crept into their hiding places and killed them brutally.

She then flitted to the fitting rooms, to my sister's camp. Ariel hadn't been asleep either, but she'd been lying down, turned over on her side so the camera couldn't catch the fact that her eyes were open. Naturally, Jeena had assumed she was asleep too, and come to finish her off and become the victor.

I watch the replay in fascinated terror.

Jeena started to crawl into my sister's fitting room through the empty space underneath the door. Little did she know, Ariel had grabbed a kitchen knife from the housewares department downstairs and hidden it under a pile of blankets acting as a pillow. The moment Jeena tried to creep in, she only managed to slip one hand inside before Ariel dropped the tip of the knife with astonishing precision, severing three of Jeena's fingers in one swipe.

Emergency medics had swarmed the place in the blink of an eye. I watch it all play out, watch the fast-paced scenes I had no idea were happening while I was asleep. Jeena's hand was patched up. She was given salves and medicine, then questioned about her intentions. When asked if she wanted to continue in the tournament or drop out now, she simply glared with her evil eyes, at the inquirer, at the camera, at everything, and answered with that same line from before: *I will be the next Influencer.*

Once the playback finishes, the live stream cuts back to the present moment, to the happenings of now. My sister is safe as always in her little cubby. The blood stains from

Jeena's fingers have been wiped from the fitting room floor; now it gleams without a single stain or blemish. Ariel munches casually on some food she got from one of the restaurants in the food court. She is safe, for now.

But I know Jeena will want her dead more than ever now. She'll no longer just have the hunger of winning, but the desire for revenge. Still, I am hopeful. Against all expectations, Ariel has survived nearly the entire week. She only needs to last twenty-four more hours.

In Jeena's neck of the woods, things seem relatively normal. She is posting as always, racking in more and more likes and followers. The only thing that has changed is that she keeps her wounded hand down and out of the shot every time she snaps a picture. She hides her infirmity, keeping her face as wildly happy and perky as ever. Still, I see the lust for my sister's blood in her gaze. I see the truth there. The ugly, cold truth.

She'll be plotting her next twenty-four hours very carefully, too carefully, maybe. Planning not only her own path to victory, but a way to eradicate Ariel as well. I shudder to think what must be going through my sister's head right now. She's surprised me with her ingenuity, with her cleverness. But I still look at her and see a vulnerable six-year-old.

I worry she is terrified out of her wits, and lonely. I wish I could hug her, wish I could burst through the screen and save her. If it wasn't for the CEO of HXT forcing everyone's focus onto advancing the technologies of social media, our world might have progressed enough to invent teleportation. But since such fantasies are far from our reality of poverty, all I can do for my sister is root her on silently, praying and hoping she takes it all.

———

I really need to utilize my day off by cleaning the house or doing something productive, but I'm glued to my device all day.

In between checking my sister's ranking to see how she's faring in terms of follower count, I watch the live stream like it holds the promise of bestowing fortune and fame on me. I guess, in a way, it does. Only if Ariel wins, though.

But for the rest of the day, there is no clear indication of who will be the winner. Both Ariel and Jeena keep to themselves, eyeing each other's movements from their own devices when they're not busy boosting their online presence. Though they both know where the other is at any given moment, neither of them go after the other. They stay in their spaces, Ariel in the fitting room on the second floor, Jeena in the basement with the bedding and furniture. For a while, the tournament is actually *boring.* I'm able to sit my phone down for a couple hours and do some laundry that had piled up.

But then, around three in the afternoon, something happens. Something *changes.*

Both girls, at the same time, run out of their food stocks.

They're both starving.

And they *both* head to the food court to replenish their stash.

For a moment, they stand on opposite ends of the court, watching each other with the tensed stances of animals. Jeena, I notice, has a knife clutched in her hand. But so does Ariel. Either of them could charge at the other, or toss their weapon over the long-abandoned tables and chairs.

But no one moves.

Then, slowly, Jeena takes the first step. She moves at an

angle, inching toward a restaurant that used to serve pizza and Italian food. Most of the food is probably gone, and any remaining is probably rotted. But she might be able to find something in a can. She creeps that way, and finally, my sister moves. Seeing that, for the moment, she is safe.

Ariel darts in the opposite direction, to an empty Chinese place. The camera shows each of them gathering their respective nourishments before running back to their hiding spots without even glancing once at each other.

Long after the two of them are safe in their camps again, something occurs to me.

It seems weird that Jeena didn't even *try* to attack my sister. She has already proven, by killing every other contestant, that she is brutal and not afraid to use violence. So, why didn't she ambush Ariel the way she did the others? Why did she hesitate?

Even though my sister has proven to be cleverer than I realized she was, there is no doubt in my mind that, in a fight, Jeena would win. She had all the power to pounce on my sister and come out victorious. And she knew that, as well. There was no fear in her eyes when she looked at Ariel, no anxiety at being attacked. *She* knew she was superior just as well as I knew it.

Still, she held back.

Why? It doesn't make sense.

I worry about it for hours, but thankfully, nothing happens for the rest of the day.

THERE WAS A TIME WHEN MY SISTER *DIDN'T* CARE ABOUT becoming an Influencer. Even though I pray she wins the tournament, I wish I could resurrect those long-gone days and turn her back into the carefree child she once was.

Back then, she used her phone to play games and send me silly messages. She didn't even have HXT installed, or any other social platform. She was just a kid.

So much has changed now. I miss the old Ariel. But the new Ariel is better than *no* Ariel. If she dies, my whole world will shatter. For a while, I am overcome with emotion, with fear over what may happen tonight.

But at least I know, no matter what the outcome is, this whole thing will be over tomorrow. After tonight, I won't have to wonder anymore — and that, at least, is a comfort.

Chapter 6

The alarm wrenches my eyes open with its shrill scream at eight o'clock. I wake up with lead in my limbs. Today is the day my life will come to an end. I'm sure of it. That as soon as I turn on my device, I'll find the news that Jeena has brutally murdered my sister in the middle of the night and taken the victor's crown as the sixtieth annual tournament winner.

I am already bracing myself as I throw my legs over the side of my lumpy bed and drag myself out from under the thin, worn blanket. For a moment, I look at that blanket that has never provided any warmth, and wonder if I'll be trading it out for a thick, lush one later today. But I shake my head of that ridiculous thought, refusing to even let myself dream.

There's no way. There's simply no way Ariel has won.

Though I know what I'll find, I'm dreading seeing my fears confirmed. I turn on my phone and click on the live stream.

And I am instantly shocked.

The first thing I see is this: a group of armed guards

leading two people out of the abandoned mall into the gray light of morning outside. The two people are the last two contestants. Jeena and Ariel — neither of them have killed in the middle of the night, and now the competition has finished with *two*.

"This has never happened before," I whisper to myself just as the hostess, who moves into the camera's focus, makes the same declaration.

"In all sixty years of the tournament, this has *never* happened!" She says, smiling once for the billions of viewers, then again at Jeena and Ariel, who stand arm to arm with the guards flanking their sides. They look just as bewildered as I feel, especially my sister, whose warm dark-blue eyes are practically bulging out of her head.

Every other tournament, the winner has always been clear. The Saturday night before the competition ends at eight that Sunday morning has always been known as Butcher Night, because people are always eager to finish off their opponents before the morning dawns, in order to secure their own victory.

I had been sure that Jeena would come in the night like Jack the Ripper and utterly destroy Ariel. But she hadn't. And Ariel hadn't done anything to Jeena, either. They'd both just stayed in their private camps the whole night.

And now… now what?

The hostess grins into her microphone and says, "Wow, this continues to be our most intense tournament to date! Normally, if a situation like this ever arose, we would decide the winner based on which of the two has the most followers. But I've just been told a critical point: both Ariel and Jeena have nine hundred million followers! It's a *tie!*"

A tie? Seriously?

I sink back down onto the bed with a sigh. Great. There is no telling what they'll do to break this tie. I am tempted to hope that Ariel will win, but I don't let myself. Not yet.

"Listen up, viewers. Here's what we're going to do." The hostess gives the camera a somber look as she drops this announcement. I, and everyone else in the world, hang onto her every word. "We're going to have our crowning ceremony at noon today, like we do every year. But instead of crowning a victor who has already won, we will be *choosing* the winner. Both girls will come up on stage, and the winner will be picked based on the amount of followers they have gained in the next four hours. Let me say it again, world. You have *four hours* to choose the winner of the Sixtieth Annual Influencer Tournament! Whoever reaches one *billion* followers by twelve o'clock, or close to it, will receive the crown and glory. Now, as tradition dictates, the ceremony will take place in the winner's hometown. But since there isn't a winner yet, we'll toss a smartphone to pick the location."

In the olden days, before smartphones were made indestructible by literally *any* means, people would have balked at the thought of throwing their phones up into the air and letting them crash down on concrete. They would have, instead, flipped a coin, an ancient ritual that went out of fashion over seventy years ago. But the principles between the two are the same. With coin tossing, you either have a heads outcome or a tails outcome. With smartphone tossing, it is either the front camera or the back camera.

The hostess pulls out her own phone and holds it dramatically as she lifts her eyes to both girls.

"Jeena," she says, "as the oldest, you pick first. Front camera or back camera?"

"Front," Jeena says.

Her eyes are steely, her tone grim and reserved. There

is none of the usual glamorous bravado that she'd boasted all throughout the week.

"That gives you the back camera, Ariel," the hostess says.

Ariel gives a serious nod.

Then the hostess flicks her wrist and sends her smartphone hurtling into the air. The camerawork catches all of its frantic, spinning spirals before zeroing in on its dramatic downward plunge. A second later, the phone crashes onto the ground, a bad fall, but not harmful. At first, it lands on its back, with the front camera facing the camera. But then the phone bounces on the cement, does another flip, and lands on the opposite end. Its back camera faces upward. Ariel has won.

"Excellent!" the hostess cries, just as my little sister starts to beam. "That settles it then. Today's crowning ceremony will take place in Ariel's hometown, the capital of New California. Remember folks, you have until twelve noon to decide the world's next Influencer."

The camera then pans to Ariel and Jeena as they are led to a pair of black vans that have just pulled up to the curb. In keeping with tradition, the girls will be driven to the airport, where they will be flown from wherever the competition's secret location is to the capital of New California. I don't know where they'll go from there, but I'm assuming they'll be taken to a hotel room and given hair stylists and beauticians to prepare them for the ceremony. Like every year, it will probably take place in City Hall.

Having nothing more to show, at least for the next four hours anyway, the live stream ends, but is replaced by a 168-hour long playback of the past seven days. I don't understand why they always do that. Everyone in the entire world has already watched the tournament live. Why would they want to see it again? Why would any sane person want to relive nine — or in this case, *eight* — brutal murders?

It's beyond me, but I don't waste time trying to figure it out. For the first time throughout the entire competition, I am bursting with hope. I, actually, truly *believe* my sister can take the grand prize. It isn't just wishful thinking now — the hope inside me is so tangible I feel as though it's as real as another organ nestled inside my body.

So, I spend the rest of the morning lost in preparations. I pull three packs of the lab-produced hamburger patties from the freezer and set them out on the counter with the mind to make Ariel a special homecoming dinner. Then I go to her room with a couple of giant garbage bags, the poor man's suitcase, and start filling them with all her stuff.

Ariel doesn't have many possessions, and I know she'll be gifted a whole new wardrobe and a bedroom full of fancy stuff once she wins. But I still want to pack all of her stuff, all the old toys she still kept from childhood, all the photographs that are creased and bent and faded, all the awards and trophies she got from doing well in school, before social media took over her life.

But now, it's all about to pay off, I can *feel* it. All the sleepless nights worrying about her, all the anguish from watching her kill herself on exercise machines and diets — it will all be worth it now. She will get to go over the Wall, her greatest dream. And I will be able to go with her.

Chapter 7

At twenty till noon, there is a knock on my door. When I go to answer it, I am surprised to find the man and the limousine waiting there, just beyond my doorstep. He tells me that, as a member of Ariel's immediate family, I am granted a personal escort to the ceremony. Wow. Fancy.

As the limousine door is opened for me, and I am helped into the sleek, spacious backseat, I wonder if this is going to be my future from now on, if I should get used to such extravagance. I've never even owned a car, and now, I'm riding in one of the most expensive ones.

All because of social media. All because of the tournament. All because of HXT and its enigmatic CEO.

I wonder if she'll be there, at the ceremony, as I'm riding through town on a cushioned seat even softer than my own mattress. My wonder is mostly doubt, though. She's never made an appearance at any of the tournament ceremonies. Sure, this year's has quickly gone down in history, but it's still highly unlikely that she'll make an appearance.

For some reason, she insists upon protecting her privacy, which is ironic considering the empire she created revolves around cameras, socializing, and transparency.

In the limousine, there are meals and beverages I have never even heard of before. Salty, crunchy discs, which the driver tells me are called "potato chips." Some kind of legumes known as "honey-roasted peanuts." And a sparkling drink, which is bitter and sweet at the same time, and makes my head spin. I take a few sips before setting it down.

"Champagne," the driver tells me.

I tell him I'm not a fan, and he laughs.

Then the car stops, and outside the window by my face, I can see, clearly, the tall building made of stone. City Hall stands out like an island, a refuge. It is the cleanest place in the city, as well as the biggest. The front façade has been decorated with brightly colored string and big banners.

On the green lawn out front, two dozen chairs have been set up. The scene reminds me of ancient footage of outdoor amphitheaters and the concerts held at them. Nowadays, the only people privileged enough to have celebrities come and perform for them are those who live over the Wall.

The front row of chairs has been reserved for the family of the contestants. I don't know how they found out my name and the fact that I was Ariel's only family, but her end of the chairs is the shortest one: only one seat. The other five in the row are taken up with Jeena's family, who look sleepy and jetlagged from the plane trip they had to endure to get here. I sit next to a little boy with glossy black hair, who must be her younger brother, and then stare up at the stone podium as Mayor Hawkins rises to take his position in the center of it.

"Good afternoon, everyone," he greets.

He speaks into a microphone attached to the podium, and his voice booms around us. He's a mousy man with a round stomach and an even rounder bald head, but his cadence is deep and thundering. He is the only one in the town wealthy enough to afford a house with two levels and the crisp black suit stretching taut over his body.

"Thank you all for coming," he continues, "and thank you to the camera crew for filming all this live, so everyone around the world can watch even though they can't be with us in person. This is quite a momentous occasion. This is the first time in all sixty years of the tournament that one of this sleepy little town's residents has gotten this close to winning the whole competition. We are very proud of our own Ariel Eckert. But before we bring her out, along with Jeena, we have a very special guest here with us to give the pre-crowning speech."

Several people behind me cheer. This is one of those things that people in the Ordinary World look forward to every year. They get a kick out of watching the crowning ceremonies and finding out who the surprise celebrity will be giving the speech. Last year, it was Dom Johnson, a pop musician who briefly went public with the world-renowned Influencer, Loren Harper. But their relationship didn't last long before Harper declared Dom a lying, cheating jerk in one of her TenSec videos, and proclaimed their union dead to twenty billion viewers before even telling *him*.

Who will the surprise guest be now?

I listen to people whisper their speculations behind me. Several of them — teenage girls mostly — mention Adam Ridley. I know him, of course, but I'm not impressed by him. He appears in a lot of commercials promoting a certain type of juice that has apparently "made him what he is." But what he is isn't that special, just a smooth-skinned sixteen-year-old with a nose ring and a flop of thick hair he frequently dyes a myriad of wild colors.

Frankly, there isn't anyone I would be too excited to see. The only celebrities I somewhat like are all dead, ghosts from the Old World. People with imaginations, with talent, interests that went beyond follower count. People like Tim Burton or Michael Jackson.

After teasing the audience for a moment, Mayor Hawkins flings his arm out in a flourish and finally announces the guest: "Everyone, please welcome… Loren Harper!"

The crowd goes nuts as the door to the City Hall opens, and a girl steps out into the sunlight. The ground beneath me vibrates from the herd of stamping feet. My ears ring from the blaring shouts and cheers. If there is one person who is loved by *everyone* in this world — men, women, elderly, children — it's Loren Harper.

She steps onto the podium in heels and a bouncy, flowery dress that shows off her "ideal" body and probably costs more than my three weeks' wages. Her hair is buttercup-gold and hangs in long, thick waves down her shoulders. Her skin is what every girl pines after: dewy, tan, and blemish-free.

She wears light makeup, because Loren is one of those rarities with natural beauty. Or so everyone online says. I look at her closely, and decide that they're right. Here, with her simple mascara and clear lip gloss, she looks more *real* than the Barbie they show on all the cosmetic commercials. She also is very pretty.

As I am in the front row, just a yard or two away from her, I have a perfect view of her height, which would be tall even without the pink heels strapped to her feet, her soft rose-pink cheeks, and her eyes, which are an uncommon shade of rock crystal green. They lock onto mine for a brief, chest-tightening moment before flitting to every other face in the crowd. She is a charmer, the kind of person who boasts humility and kindness, beauty along with a sweet, girl-next-door personality. I can see why all of Earth is smitten with her.

How old is she? I wonder.

I bet her parents are so proud of the diamond they produced, of the perfect life her star-quality allowed them to have.

"Hey, everyone. I'm Loren Harper," she declares, as if nobody knows, which is laughable.

Though it has been roughly a decade since she won the tournament and moved to her new home over the Wall, she still talks with the faint southern accent indigenous to her hometown in New Tennessee. Her voice lilts when she speaks, and it's endearing. Everyone beams at her as if she's promising money and healing to all of us and our children.

"It's crazy to think it's already been ten years since I won this competition myself," she says. "Back then, I was barely fifteen years old, and I'd only had social media for a few months. It's insane to think that so many people like me, and continue to like me after all these years. Frankly, I don't understand. I'm just that skinny little kid from New Tennessee, deep down inside. And I'm humbled and grateful for the wonderful, beautiful life all of your love has provided for me."

She takes a moment to smile at everyone, and again, her eyes stop on mine. For a moment, I am entranced as her eyes don't immediately flit away. Instead, they linger for a second or two longer than they did on any other face. My stomach gives a weird lurch. Am I hungry? Should I have eaten those snacks in the limousine?

Then her eyes leave me, onto the next person, and she continues her speech.

"Every year, I enjoy watching the tournament myself. It is exciting to get to know the new generation of Influencers. But this season was by far the best. I was so invested in finding out what happened between Jeena and Ariel that I may have, secretly, neglected a photo shoot or two."

She blushes, and the crowd shrieks at this display of bashfulness. Meanwhile, I am grinning and anticipating the death of my little sister's heart that surely ensued when she heard her number one idol say her name.

After the buzz dies down, Loren finishes, "So, it gives me great pleasure to introduce the two finalists of the Sixtieth Annual Next Influencer Tournament... Jeena Lee and Ariel Eckert!"

The City Hall door opens again, and to joyous cheers, my sister steps out first.

I've never seen her look so glamorous. The beautifiers she must have received in her hotel room seemed to have worked a certain magic on her face, which is almost *glowing*, as if her skull bears its own private sun beaming its rays through the rest of her face. Her lips are smooth and glossy pink, her eyes are lined with dark blue pigment that makes her sapphire eyes look like they were colored with a crayon.

She smiles at everyone in the crowd, waving her hand like a princess. Her gaze lands on my face, and instantly, both of our eyes are swimming with tears. She looks away the same time I look down — avoiding each other to keep from bawling like babies.

Then she moves to stand on one side of Loren, looking absolutely starstruck.

"Congratulations, Ariel," Loren says into her mic, addressing both my sister and the viewers.

"T-Thank you," my sister replies in a timid voice when Loren holds the microphone under her chin.

Everyone in the audience goes "aww" at the same time, and then the door opens for the last time, bringing out the person that reduces everyone to total silence.

When Jeena click-clacks out onto the podium in her spiked high heel shoes, it's as if her presence pulled a trigger to release a thick blanket from the sky. The blanket smothers all noise in the atmosphere. Nobody even breaths as they watch the deadliest contestant in all sixty years of the tournament step up on Loren's other side.

"Congratulations, Jeena," Loren says to the girl.

Her tone is different when she addresses Jeena, I notice. More formally polite, not as sweet as the way she talked to my sister. I wonder if Ariel notices.

Loren turns back to face the crowd, and the first face her eyes land on is my own.

I don't know why I blush. Harper *is* an attractive girl, not nearly as gross and glittery as most of the famous Influencers. But it's silly for my stomach to lurch when she looks at me. Her eyes flit away soon anyway, onto someone else. She's polite, kind, meeting everyone's eyes.

Then she announces, "Well, everyone, it's officially twelve-noon. Both Jeena and Ariel's social media profiles have been briefly halted, allowing no more comments, likes, or followers, until the winner is chosen. Let's take a look at the final numbers to see which of the girls will be this year's victor!"

A hologram appears, hovering midair behind Harper's head. That's another one of the Influencer World luxuries. All of us here in the Ordinary World are still living archaically with our smartphones and other handheld devices. Many Influencers use them too, but there also exists an advanced technology that the majority of them get to enjoy: *holograms.* I am amazed to see it, but too nervous to pay much attention to it. It's the results my eyes are focused on.

The screen projected onto thin air is massive, stretching from one end of City Hall's front façade to the other. It glows with blue light, like most smartphones, but it is bigger, crisper, brighter. Almost too bright. I squint my eyes against the glare and watch the number *10* appear on the screen. It quickly changes to *9.* A countdown begins, led by Loren, and joined by every other voice in the crowd.

8… 7… 6…

I meet my sister's eyes for a second time. This time, neither of us cry. We smile at each other. I mouth: *I'm proud of you.* She mouths back: *I love you.*

5…4…

My heart pounds. My fingers shake so much I'm surprised they haven't fallen off yet.

3…2…1!

The first thing my eyes lock onto are the numbers by Ariel's name. *No. of Likes: 35 billion. No. of Comments: 800 million. Followers: 50 billion.*

Then, swiftly, moving like lightning, my eyes shift below her name to Jeena's.

No. of Likes: 34 billion. No. of Comments: 789 million. Followers: 46 billion.

My chest tightens. For ten whole seconds, I don't take in a single breath of oxygen.

Then the screen blacks out. The hologram disappears.

Loren declares in a voice that rings out over the entire town, the entire world: "And the winner is… *Jeena!*"

WHAT?

Loren turns to place a crown on Jeena's head. Her

family jolts up out of their chairs, cheering, screaming, rushing toward their smiling daughter.

But the rest of the crowd doesn't even give a single clap. Everyone is silent. Everyone saw what I saw. Ariel, my sister, won! Her numbers were higher than Jeena's! How the hell can they say Jeena is the winner, when the results are there in black and white?

After a second, I get my wits together and rise to my feet. I feel my face, contorting into an expression of rage. Ariel alights from the podium with glumness in every line of her face; dejectedly, she eyes the ground as she walks toward me. But my eyes are on Loren Harper, watching with disgust as she chats jovially with Jeena's family, her joyous smile just as overdone as the one they show on all the commercials.

In a fit of fury, I yell out, "What the hell do you think you're doing?"

The excited chatter coming from Jeena and her family dies down. Everyone on the podium — Jeena, her parents, her little brother, and Loren — all look at me. The atmosphere itself seems to be holding its breath. Everyone in the chairs around me has quieted to the point of muteness; it's as if they're no longer there at all.

Loren meets my infuriated eyes with her calm ones. "Yes?"

I jab a finger toward the empty air that had, for one second, held the holographic screen. "Didn't any of you read the results? *Ariel* was the one with the highest results, not *her.*"

With blank, paralyzed faces, everyone looks at me.

Then — a voice behind me gasps: "My gosh, the Internet is going *crazy*!"

I whip around to face the woman who spoke. She is poring over her smartphone with wide eyes. Like a madman, I snatch it from her without even asking, and in a quick, sweeping glance of the screen and the millions of comments displayed on it, I can get the gist of how the world is feeling.

Nobody is congratulating Jeena. *Everyone* is talking about Ariel. I'm not the only one enraged by this.

With the same, identical twitch of their hands, every other person in the audience whips out their phone. They all look at the comments, see what people are saying.

And what are they saying? Well, amongst other impassioned obscenities written in all-caps, a common sentiment that appears in nearly every comment is the fact that the competition was *rigged.*

Rigged? That's a word that's never been used in the tournament before.

I read on, soaking in the world's theories.

This is a joke!

Jeena was rigged to win all along!

Why do you think she never got killed or never had to sleep? She probably had protections and 24/7 awake pills snuck in for her.

She probably knows someone over the Wall.

Anger bubbles up inside me, a volcano preparing to blow. I throw the woman back her phone, then swivel around to face the podium, and the people still posed on it in shock. None of them have moved.

I narrowed my eyes. "They're saying Jeena was rigged to win. Is that true?"

Loren's eyes widen. I can tell her expression is genuine. If the tournament *was* rigged, Loren knows nothing about it.

Jeena's face, on the other hand, does not look so innocent.

She's smirking. In the span of two seconds, that smirk becomes a grin, which shifts into a full-blown evil cackle.

"So, what if it is rigged?" she laughs. "It's not like anything can be done about it now! *I* have the victor's crown!"

With that, she points at the glittering tiara on her head, and my fists clench with an urge to rip it off her skull.

I'm so mad I'm practically having a seizure from the waves of rage ricocheting through me. Memories flash through my mind, taking me on a rollercoaster ride back through the tournament footage of the past week. I recall the last day, remember why the usually ruthless Jeena was being so easy on my sister. I'd thought it strange that she didn't want to get cold-blooded revenge for having her finger chopped off.

But now, I understand. Now, I know the reason for her calm avoidance. She was never afraid of my sister. She just knew she had this whole thing in the bag.

One… two… three… four…

I try to count to ten, try to take deep breaths. But my indignation is not so easily diffused.

"Who is it then?" I bark at her, raising my voice over the nervous murmurs that have started to creep through the crowd. "Who are you in cahoots with over the Wall?"

Jeena gives a slick, sly smile in response. "My older sister Minji. She's the makeup artist for HXT's CEO's daughter."

"Wait a second." The anger deepens. "You're telling me that that blasted CEO was *in on it?*"

Maddeningly, Jeena just shrugs, smiling, and reaches a hand up to lovingly stroke the jewels encrusted in her crown.

I can barely think straight, can barely comprehend all of this.

Fury on my sister's behalf consumes me.

All I know is that I want to kill the CEO of HXT with my bare hands.

But since she's not here… that smirking little girl with the crown on her head will suffice just fine.

I have never been violent. I never even enjoyed those murderous video games all the guys played growing up. But when I think about Ariel, who has wasted upwards of five years on this flimsy dream of hers, and she finally *almost* gets it, but then gets it ripped out from under her by a witch with connections… I can't even describe to you the rage.

But I can describe what it makes me do.

Before I'm even conscious of making the decision, I find myself running, rushing toward the stage. My hands are outstretched, but I haven't decided yet what to do with them. Should I wring her neck? Claw her eyes out? Or just give her the same brutal treatment she gave all the contestants? Taste of her own medicine might be nice.

I run toward the horrified, paralyzed faces before me — and I'm almost there… but at the last second, just when Jeena is staring wide-eyed at me like a helpless squirrel caught in the path of an oncoming semi-truck, Loren Harper dives in front of her, arms out, and I am forced to a screeching halt.

Briefly, I register her frightened, childlike eyes and her hair fluttering as a gust of wind rolls across the lawn. But then I just fling her aside, out of my way. There is a collective gasp behind me as everyone in the audience sucks a breath, watching Loren's fall. She drops to the grass, and the sound of her impact rings out like metal instead of the earthy thump I expected. Strange, but it doesn't bother me too much. Because in a second, she shoots up again, totally unharmed despite that fall, and she's rushing at me.

But I'm already gone. Running straight to the Lee family.

Jeena is shielded by her mom, who's shielded by her father. At this point, I am so enraged I don't even care that this man is not my original target. He should not be the one escorting someone over the Wall. That should be my job. I pull my arm back, and then send a whopping fist into his face.

That's what does it. That tiny little punch, that one act of violence, is the catalyst that sets everyone in motion. My fight with Jeena's father incites twenty other fights as people in the crowd, some on Jeena's side, others on Ariel's, are pitted against each other. Riots break out, people screaming out for justice and fairness. I almost grin bitterly at that request, knowing it will never happen. Not in this world. Not while social media exists. Not while the Wall that separates us is up.

Jeena's father, who looks portly and aging at first, is surprising me with his fighting skills. I thought he would be easy to take down, but he's nailing just as many punches as I am. I think, fleetingly, as his fist is whipping out to slam me in the gut, that he must have trained in martial arts.

But then I am on the ground, bleeding, and for the moment, all I am conscious of is the intense pain. Through blurry eyes, I see Jeena's father hovering over me. His face is unsure. He looks like he wants to hit me some more, but like he thinks he may have hit me too hard at the same time.

I turn my head, see the riots. I'm not the only one bleeding on the floor. Many other people have been beaten to death. Literally. I wince, the sight of the blood and corpses on the City Hall front lawn even more painful than my actual wounds. They're going to destroy each other. They're really, actually, going to—

Wait. Where's Ariel?

I worry I've remembered my sister too late. I can't let her be part of this mess. I can't risk her being attacked, or worse…

At this horrifying thought, I shoot up. Worry for Ariel consumes every other emotion inside me. It even overpowers the physical pain. I whip around, my eyes scanning the chaos for her familiar face. But I don't see her. Anywhere.

And she's not the only one missing. I notice, with confusion, that Loren Harper is gone, too.

That can't be a coincidence, can it?

I don't understand what's happened, but I'm comforted by the fact that their bodies are nowhere to be seen. That's a good sign, right?

A horrible scream shoots into the air, and I turn, already dreading the sight of Ariel being assaulted. But it isn't my sister. It's Jeena and her family. They're mobbed by the Ariel supporters. It only takes a second for blood to start flying.

I turn away from the sight, squeeze my eyes shut. Even though I have seen many murders take place over the course of that week, it has all been through a screen. Nothing is more disturbing than watching killings happen in person, mere feet from you. I wish I could stand there forever with my eyes shut, tuning all this out.

But suddenly, I feel a hand snatch up mine, and someone tugs me forward. It happens so fast. Before I've even fully opened my eyes, the shrieks and riot noises are cut off. The warm air is replaced with icy cold air.

I open my eyes, again, expecting to see Ariel. So, I am surprised when I see three strangers there, staring at me. One is a tall man who towers over me both in height and personality. He's got a strong, formidable presence, like a cop or someone who was in the military. He's the one who grabbed me. Now, he removes his hand.

The other person looks to be his wife. She's a petite woman with graying blonde hair, and as she clings to his side, I see the black fear in her eyes.

The third person is a curly-haired teenage boy, their son, by the looks of it.

And where have they brought me? I look around, finding tall stone pillars, vaulted ceilings, and gleaming tile floors instead of blood-stained grass, overcast skies, and empty streets.

Oh. I'm in the City Hall building.

But why?

"What's going on?" I ask.

In the back of my mind, I'm more disturbed by the diminishment of the noise outside, more so than I was by the screams. That means there are less throats to produce sound. More bodies dead on the ground.

The man looks at me, earnestly. They all do. His wife, son — all three of them fix their eyes on me with an imploring expression, like they've got something they want to beg me to do, but are already anticipating I'll say no to.

"My name is Rick," the man says.

"I'm Elle," the woman adds.

"And I'm Greg," the teenage boy finishes.

"We're the Dohertys," the odd man continues. "And you are Ariel's brother, correct? Zachary Eckert?"

"How did you know that?" I demand, narrowing my eyes.

At this point, I am suspicious of everyone. How many people are secretly tied to the power-hungry, bloodthirsty enigma that is HXT's CEO?

"I reckon everyone in this town knows who you are," Rick Doherty says with a short, mirthless laugh. "When your sister got picked, news spread like wildfire in the factory."

"You work in the factory?" I've never seen him before, so I instantly doubt this information.

But Rick just snorts at me, as if I'm a dumb child questioning the truth of an indisputable fact, like the Earth being round or something.

He tells me, "There's more to the factory than just the ground floor. The wife and I both work on the upper levels — where chargers and earbuds are assembled. Plus, I knew your father. Worked for him as a boy, some odd forty years ago, back when there was still need for mechanics and landscapers and… well, anyway, there's no time to bore you with the past. The point is, I know you, and now you know us. We've got to hurry if this is going to work."

"If *what* is going to work?"

Now it's Elle's turn to explain. She jumps into the conversation, starting with a confession.

"We're rebels." And she says it as if there were a capital R on the word *rebel*, like they were an organization or something. "We have been thoroughly building our plan to overthrow the Influencer World for over a decade."

Chapter 8

"**W**hat?!"

This isn't just shocking. This is earth-shattering. I've never met another person who questioned or voiced dislike for the way our world was run. Is this strange family serious? Or is this all part of a weird test?

"Let us explain, dear," the kindly-faced woman says, laying a calming hand to my shoulder. She has thick silver hair that reminds me of ancient images of a legendary woman called Mrs. Claus. "In the beginning, when the Wall was first being built, much of the world was against it. They clung to the old-world values of togetherness, and hated the thought of separating everyone, especially on the basis of something as flimsy as online popularity. So, many rebel groups were formed. Rick's parents were part of one of the original ones."

"But then," Rick interjects, "when the Influencers started posting and doing commercials about how great life over the Wall was, most people shifted their focus. Instead of resisting the Wall and the world beyond it, now, their obsession was *joining* the people over the Wall. Becoming an

Influencer. Most of the rebel groups dissolved within a year. But my family continued to hold stubbornly to their determination, and they instilled those same values into me. I grew up surrounded by plans and blueprints and secret meetings. Naturally, I took over when my parents died, and when I met Elle, her and I continued the overthrow plan. But the situation looked bleak, because we knew we would only be able to make a difference if we could actually get *over* the Wall, which is impossible for Ordinaries, except for one day every year."

"The tournament," I gasp.

The whole family starts smiling and nodding at me.

"Yes," Elle confirms. "Once we realized we could use the tournament to our advantage, we shifted our plans in that direction. Since then, we came up with this blueprint."

Out of her jean pocket, she withdraws a tiny piece of paper the size of a small cube. It looks like it has been folded over a thousand times. When she unfolds it, I am astounded by the intricate design imprinted on the paper. It is an old-fashioned blueprint, a map, showing a web of lines and other details for the plan they've formed.

The Wall is clearly drawn and marked, and so is a helicopter sitting off in the right upper corner of the paper. There is also a faceless stick figure labeled *Winner* that I assume must refer to the tournament victor. I gape at the blueprint in shock and awe for a minute before raising my eyes to Elle's once more.

"How long have you had this plan?"

"Over a decade."

"How come you haven't done it yet then?"

"Because there's a key element that has to be done *just right*; otherwise, the plan will never work."

"What's the key element?" I ask.

Rick answers, "The tournament winner."

"You see," Elle says, "step one of the plan is actually getting over the Wall. In order to do that, we have to infiltrate the only vehicle that ever carries people from the Ordinary World to the Influencer World."

"The winner's helicopter," I say with a nod of understanding.

"Yes. But the helicopter is small. There's no way of us stowing away in the back unseen. This is where the problem comes in. We have already factored in the fact that we'll probably have to kill the pilot — or at least, drug him. But that leaves us with the winner. And unless the winner is the *right* winner, they would probably instantly alert us to the authorities and ruin our plan in a second."

"Wait, what do you mean 'the right winner'?" I ask. "And why couldn't you just kill both the pilot and the winner?"

Elle looks horrified. "Isn't one killing enough? We may be rebels, but we are not murderous fiends like those rioters outside. The pilot murder is a necessity — killing the winner is not."

Nodding in agreement with his wife, Rick Doherty adds, "And we may not even *have* to kill the pilot. Only if he tries to contact the authorities before we have a chance to drug him. Anyway, the right winner will be someone who isn't that attached to social media or Influencer life. Someone still somewhat, well, *real*. And when we watched the tournament and discovered your sister, we *knew* she was the right winner."

"Ariel?" I gasp. "What are you talking about? Ariel has wanted to be an Influencer for years. She's just as much one of them as the rest."

Rick holds up a finger. "That is where you're wrong, son. Ariel has wanted to be an Influencer, yes. But clearly, you can see the difference between her desire for it, and Jeena's desire for it. Ariel's true want is for acceptance. Jeena just wants popularity and glamour. Ariel has depth; Jeena is heartless. It was obvious to us when we observed her resourcefulness on the show. Didn't you think it was odd that while everyone else was focused on posting and numbers, Ariel was building shelters and securing her safety? I don't know if you've seen her social profiles, but she actually uploaded a fourth of the amount of posts Jeena and the other contestants did. And yet, she won, or would have won, had things not been rigged. That was our indicator that there's more to her than a desire for fame. And of course, that will be even stronger now, since she has been wronged by social media in such a monumental way. She will be perfect for our plan."

Rick is right, about all of it. I never noticed it then, but the truth hits me now. Everything Ariel has done — going on diets, straining her body in gruesome exercise programs, buying loads of cosmetics — has never been about making huge amounts of money, living a lavish lifestyle, or having the whole planet worship her. All along, it was a cry for attention, for love. Ariel *is* real and deep and separate from the robot followers. And she *is* the perfect person for this plan.

But… I frown. Something has occurred to me.

"Wait. How will this work? Jeena's the one who will be in the helicopter, not Ariel."

"My dear boy, where was your awareness during the past thirty hours? The Lee family — all of them, including Jeena — is dead. They were killed in the mob."

I swallow. "Oh. Well, how about Ariel? I haven't been able to find her. For all I know, she could be dead, too."

"She isn't," Rick's son Greg says. "She's in the helicopter, waiting for us with Loren Harper."

"Loren?!" I shriek. "You've gotta get her out of there! Loren's probably already alerted the authorities!"

All three of the Dohertys just stare at me, something akin to sympathy in their eyes. Then, slowly, Rick begins to shake his head.

"No, Zachary. Loren Harper is a rare one too, one with a heart. We didn't expect it either, but when we noticed her leading your sister toward the helicopter, toward safety, right when the riots were becoming dangerous, we knew."

"But—"

"She rescued Ariel, Zachary," Elle Doherty adds. "Not Jeena. That says a lot, don't you think?"

I can't bring myself to reply, but she sees the answer on my face anyway.

With a nod and a sweet smile, she asks, "Now… will you be joining us?"

The air rushes out of me in a long, shaky sigh. It seems I had been holding it, squeezing it tight in my chest, without even realizing. This whole thing is insane. Literally insane.

But it also makes sense. And it's *thrilling.* And for the first time, I understand what came over me the previous day at work, what made my hands falter in the middle of assembling.

Without even knowing it (or maybe knowing all along, subconsciously), I was a rebel, too. I was one of these radicals. I have never considered myself one, but then I have never considered myself loyal to the world's system, either. Never a supporter of Influencers, never an avid Tournament watcher, never a proponent of social media. Though I never went as far as attaching the label to myself, I *have* always rebelled. Well, resisted, is more like it.

Now though… now is different. Now, having seen the influence and utter rottenness of HXT's CEO, seen bloodshed, seen my sister robbed of her future just because someone's family member did the CEO's daughter's makeup… now I will happily call myself a rebel.

Something has shifted in me, and I realize it now. I'll no longer be able to go back to the house, to the factory, quietly judging, criticizing, but mostly ignoring the division between the worlds. I'll be active now, I'll *have* to. The consuming fire inside me is demanding it. I need to get over the Wall. I need to see the never-revealed HXT CEO, face-to-face. To demand justice for Ariel. To even, perhaps, clobber her with my bare hands.

Above all, to bring the wall they've spent almost a century building up, crashing down. Literally and figuratively.

I inhale deeply, square my shoulders, and look each of the Dohertys in the eye. "Alright. I'm in."

Chapter 9

*E*verything happens very fast after that. We run out through the back doors of City Hall and end up in the dead grass outside of the building. Several yards away, the helicopter waits. Its windows face away from us, so we can't see what is happening inside.

Rick Doherty hands me a strange cylinder with a thin, sharp metal piece sticking out of the end.

"What is this?" I ask.

"A syringe. It's a medical device. We have filled it with a powerful sleep mixture."

"Where'd you get it?"

Rick says, "Elle's family used to own a pharmacy. Now, your job is to stab this man in the neck *as soon* as we have opened the helicopter door. Do not hesitate for a second, or give him any time to press a button. Make sure you push down on this thing, the plunger, so that all the fluid is released. Then, we'll pull him out of the driver's seat and lay him out on the ground. We want him to be far away when he finally wakes up. I'll pilot the helicopter."

"What if he tries something?" I ask, feeling a strange, swirling sensation in my gut — part anxiety, part thrill.

"Kill him," Rick says simply.

And then we run, darting across the lawn. The young boy, Greg, is fast. He reaches the helicopter first. There, he pauses with his hand on the pilot's door, waiting for us. I rush to his side, the syringe poised in my hand. When I'm positioned and ready, Greg yanks. The door flies open. I hear a feminine gasp but don't look to see who made the sound. My hand is already inside the helicopter, blindly jamming the needle into the man's neck. I don't even see him, don't even know what he looks like. He doesn't see me, either. But I push the plunger, sending all the medicine into his bloodstream. Within a second, he hangs his head. He's knocked out cold.

"Alright, he's out," I say.

The Dohertys busy themselves with dragging his body out of the vehicle. I let out a pent-up sigh and look at the two people in the front seats for the first time.

Though I'm seeing it with my own eyes, I still can't believe it. Rick was right. Loren really is on our side. She's there, holding my sister, who is shaky and wide-eyed, and is looking at me like she's never seen me before.

But when I say her name, her expression changes. Now, she resembles that five-year-old whose entire world was playing with her older brother, listening to the old stories he told her. With a wobble of her lower lip, she dashes from one pair of arms to another, out of Loren's embrace and into mine. When I hug her, she even *feels* like that five-year-old — small and bony. I wonder if she's hungry.

"Is there any food in here?" I ask over her shoulder.

The unconscious man is gone now. Rick Doherty now sits in the pilot's chair, and his wife and son are squeezed on the seats next to Loren.

At my question, Loren's finger lands on a button beside her. I panic at first, but to my relief, the button doesn't call authorities — it just triggers a hidden compartment, a miniature ice box, to open beside us. Loren pulls out the big rectangular box inside and holds it out for me to see.

"This is the winner's cake," she says. "It belongs to you and your sister now."

"Cake?" Ariel sniffs and leans away from me.

My sister and I have never had cake before. Such luxuries don't exist in the new world — except for over the Wall. At the smell of sugar, my stomach grumbles — so does Ariel's.

While Rick cranks on the engine, Loren passes around plates and forks that have also been prepared ahead of time. Nobody says a word as she cuts five slices of the cake — two for Ariel and me, plus one for each of the Dohertys.

Even as my sister is being handed a dessert she's only heard about in legends, she manages to frown. She's looking at Loren, noticing her idol has no slice of her own.

"You're not going to have any?" she asks.

The helicopter comes to life with a low, quiet rumble. As it lifts into the air, Loren Harper answers Ariel with a sheepish smile.

"Uh, no. I… I don't eat."

"At *all?*" Ariel gasps.

"Honey, that is ridiculous," Elle says, her maternal instincts coming out. "You *have* to eat. You'll die if you don't! Here, let me cut you a slice."

"No, it's okay." Harper chuckles, but the sound is taut. "In the Influencer sector, we're only given tablets as nourishment. They're chemically designed to satisfy hunger without containing any calories."

"How is that… how is that even possible?" I mutter aloud.

Harper shrugs.

Ariel, still ignoring her plate of cake, frowns deeper. "But… but what about all the delicious food in your guys' posts? You all go to those incredible restaurants. Just the other day, you posted that TenSec video of you and Adam Ridley eating those brownies from that café."

Harper's cheeks pink. I watch her, wondering at this strange reaction.

But then she drops three words that chill my blood. "It's all fake."

"Huh?" Ariel's eyebrows knit together.

Her hand slackens, and she nearly drops her plate of cake. I take it from her and set it down safely before she can.

Then I turn to my own slice, and start carving out my first bite while Loren begins to explain.

"Haven't you ever wondered how we're able to post about us eating all the time and yet, none of us gain an ounce?"

I pause for a second. Then slowly, keeping my eyes on her, I slide the bite of cake into my mouth.

The flavor is shocking, unlike anything I've ever tasted. I have a faint memory of eating cookies many years ago, when Mom was still alive, and before sugar became too expensive for our poverty-ridden town. Since then, I must have forgotten the taste, because the sugar overload that fills my mouth is overwhelming — overwhelmingly *delicious*. Already addicted to the taste, I quickly slice another bite and shovel it in. My cheeks bulge, but I can't get enough of the amazing flavor.

"That good, huh?" Ariel grins, watching me.

All I can do is nod and urge her with a wild hand gesture to taste it herself.

Pretty soon, Ariel has a mouth full of cake, and the

same expression on her face as I do. We chuckle at each other, at the white frosting smeared on her faces.

But the high soon wears off, and we are left in the dim wake of Loren's last words.

"Wait," Ariel says. "How can you eat it if it's fake?"

Loren shrugs. "It's engineered that way. All the restaurants and cafes serve the same fake food. But trust me — it only *looks* real. The only people who get real food are those over the Wall who *aren't* affiliated with HXT or TenSec, or any of the social media platforms. Those who are, of course, have to stay thin, but we also have to appease our fans with gorgeous visuals. And trust me, the technology is so advanced that *everything* is a gorgeous visual. But then… then you come to realize it's not what you thought."

For a moment, Harper's face, beneath the wide-eyed stares of all four of us, turns wistful. Sad. But then something shifts in her gaze. Instead of looking to be on the verge of tears, she resembles a sheepish child caught doing the exact thing her mother told her not to.

"I shouldn't be talking about this," she says.

My immediate reaction is to cast my eyes over the walls, the ceiling, every visible surface of the helicopter interior. "Why, are there microphones in here? Can they hear us? See us?"

"No, Zach," Loren says, and a shiver runs up my spine. Nobody calls me Zach, not since Mom. The feeling it spurs within me, hearing Loren say my oldest, childhood nickname, is strange. It's as if I'm standing on the edge of a cliff, and my gut is tensed up, anticipating the monstrous plunge before I even take it.

"No?" I say, wondering if she can notice how fast my heart is pounding.

"No." Loren's eyes seem shinier than normal. Wetter. I

swear I can see beads of moisture on her eyelashes — but maybe I'm just looking too closely. I lower my gaze as she continues. "It's not that we're under surveillance. It's just… everything I've told you… it's top-secret. Not only is it top-secret, but it's wrong for me to *want* to tell you. I-I'm not supposed to complain. The mindset of the Influencer World is supposed to be happy, excited, delightful."

"But it's not?" my sister whispers.

Loren doesn't answer, but she doesn't have to. The answer hangs in the air as bold as if she'd hung it by a string in the ceiling.

Silence settles over our group. We sit back in our chairs while Rick Doherty pilots the helicopter, and think. I have no idea what the others are thinking, but I'm mulling over everything Loren said. It wasn't much, but it was revealing enough. And I can't say I'm surprised. I always suspected that the biggest Influencers did a lot of pretending. Nobody can be *that* happy all the time, even if (or, sometimes, *especially*) when you have lots of wealth and glory.

But fake food? *That* I'm kind of shocked about. Not shocked that Influencers are required to stay thin, but shocked that they would go to such extreme lengths. No wonder Loren looked like she was about to start crying for a minute there.

But now though, she just looks drained. Tired. She leans back in her seat and rests her cheek in the palm of her hand. Her eyes are closed, but I don't think she's really sleeping. Just avoiding more questions probably.

For a second, I just stare at her like a stalker. I still can't believe she's actually on our side. I can't recall there ever being news of an Influencer trying to leave or revolt against their government. If there has been, it's certainly been shoved under the rug. But I have a feeling Loren will be the first. I just hope we're successful. Hope this doesn't backfire and end up thrusting horrible consequences on *her*.

She seems so young. Even though she's twenty-five, only two years my junior, there is something childlike and vulnerable about her. I never noticed before, but she has knobby knees. They click together as she shakes them. She's clearly nervous, afraid, which makes her seem even younger. I feel an urge to comfort her somehow, to tell her things are going to be okay, an empty sentiment I don't even believe myself. I doubt it would do much help for her nerves. But the impulse flares within me nonetheless.

"Alright, everyone," Rick says, "we're coming up to it. Loren? Anything I should know before landing?"

Loren snaps to attention. Her crystal-green eyes stop once on my face for the quickest of flashes before darting toward the pilot's seat.

"Um, just stop on the landing field, and wait a minute before you get out. I'll get out first. There'll be escorts there, and they'll have seen the riots on TV. I'll tell them that Jeena died during the mob, which is true. They'll go home after that. And then—"

"Really?" Rick Doherty's son Greg asks. "I thought there would be people guarding the Wall twenty-four-seven."

Loren shakes her head. "They don't need to. There's literally no way in or out."

"Wait, what?" I interrupt. "There's no way *out*?"

My stomach drops, and it has nothing to do with the steady descent the helicopter is making toward the Earth below.

"No," Loren says. "No way in or not, so no need for guards. The escorts just come out once a year to greet the tournament winner and bring them to their new house.

They'll leave as soon as I tell them the winner's dead. Once they're gone, I'll come back to the helicopter and give you guys the okay. But do not, under any circumstances, come out of here until I tell you it's safe first."

Rick and his wife nod. Ariel and I dip our heads in the same agreeing motion.

Then I ask, "What happens after we leave the helicopter?"

"Well, technically, you and your sister have a home on Influencer's Row. Right next to mine, actually. But they'll probably seal it up as soon as the news spreads, and then it'll stay empty for another year until the next winner comes. For now, you guys can stay at my place. I've got *plenty* of room."

"Really?" For some reason, the thought of staying in Loren's house makes my stomach lurch.

"But won't your family have a problem with us being there?" Ariel asks, picking nervously at a loose string on her dress. "I mean, what if they get mad and report us to the authorities?"

Loren looks down. "I live alone."

"What?" Ariel looks shocked; we all do. "You don't have a boyfriend or anything?"

Silently, Loren shakes her head.

"What about your parents?" I ask. "Don't the winner's parents always move in with them in their new house?"

"Yes. And they did." Loren lifts her eyes to mine again. Hers are dark, cold. "But they… they couldn't handle it. They're gone now."

Chapter 10

The fairytale glamour is quickly fading to reveal a grim underside.

Loren doesn't elaborate on what exactly her parents couldn't handle and where exactly they are now. But I have a creeping suspicion about what happened.

Still, there's no time to bring it up. The helicopter has landed over the Wall.

We made it.

We're actually over the Wall. The world of Ordinaries is at our backs — we're officially in Influencer territory.

I don't know whether to be excited or terrified.

"The escorts are coming," Rick says from the pilot's seat.

I follow his line of vision and look through the glass windshield. Sure enough, two burly guys in suits and dark-tinted sunglasses stride toward us from the opposite end of this wide, grassy field. Beyond this place, I see only a long stretch of asphalt leading toward a city center full of skyscrapers — buildings so tall they look like they could trample us.

But I don't get to see more because Loren hisses at me, "Get down! They might see you through the window. All of you, please, *hide*. Mr. Doherty, you might want to get out of the pilot's seat, in case they catch a glimpse of you when I open the door."

"Oh, right."

None of us question anything. We all obey Loren's orders. Elle and Greg drop to the floor first, squeezing their bodies against the far-right wall where the door is. I grab my sister's arm, and the two of us follow suit. A moment later, Rick comes and kneels down. He flattens himself into the floor between the four of us.

"Alright, I'm going," Loren announces.

From the minute she opens the door and hops down to the ground below, I'm holding my breath.

Please be safe, please be safe.

My mind chants the words automatically, though I wonder why I'm so concerned for her safety. I should be more worried about us — *we're* the trespassers here.

But what if they figure out she's a traitor? What do they do to traitors in this world?

There is so much I didn't know about the government here. So much they never told us Ordinaries. Do they even *have* a government? As far as I know, the entire world on this side of the Wall was ruled by one woman: the CEO of HXT.

Even though this has been part of my normal since birth, I still can't wrap my head around it. Why should a social media mogul be an entire continent's leader? In the old-world days, nations were led by politicians. There were presidents and senators. There were parties like Democrats and Republicans. People were divided based on their political values, not on whether they had an Internet following or not.

Suddenly, the helicopter door swings open, and everyone hiding on the floor flinches for one second.

But then, the smell of rose-scented perfume touches our noses. We lift our heads and sigh in relief. It's just Loren. But is she here with good news? I can't tell. The kid's got a good poker face.

"What happened?" Rick asks, slowly rising into a sitting position.

The rest of us follow his lead.

"It worked," Loren says simply. "I told them about the riots, about Jeena dying. They went back to their homes. They asked if I wanted to be escorted to mine. I told them to go on ahead, and that I have to get my things out of the helicopter."

"So… they're gone now?" I ask.

Loren nods. "Yup. They're gone."

"So… can we get out now?" It's Rick's teenage son who asks this question; I can see the impatience in every line of his young face.

"Yes," Loren says. "But… I have to warn you. It's not what you guys think. Just… don't be shocked, okay?"

We all frown at her, but nod anyway.

Then one by one, we alight from the helicopter.

My feet touch down on the ground below. But the feeling is not what I expected.

The grass doesn't feel like normal grass. It feels… springy. Like the trampolines from the old world. Instead of walking across solid, bumpy Earth, I feel like I'm trekking across a plane of mattresses. Only Loren has a serene, emotionless expression on her face. The others around me hold the same bewildered face. This is weird. This can't be real ground.

But none of us mention it.

Not mattresses. No, that's not a good way to describe it. It's more like… stage furniture. Like a prop for a play.

Loren leads the way. After a moment, the grass field ends and makes way for a strip of black asphalt. The road feels the same way as the grass. Plastic and springy. *Fake.* Something about it makes a chill run down my spine.

"Welcome to the Capitol," Loren announces.

Just as she says it, the scenery changes abruptly. Skyscrapers emerge from around a bend up ahead. The city unfurls before us, but it's not the bright, bustling, party scene I expected. Certainly not the one depicted in every corner of social media. The Capitol of the Influencer World is supposedly the Mecca of all things happy, exciting, and bursting with people and possibilities.

But the city we step into is barely a city at all. It's a ghost town. It's just an empty strip of empty road and tall, empty buildings looming over us.

"Is anyone actually *in* those buildings?" Ariel asks in a small voice.

"Well, sometimes," Loren admits. "But it depends on the day. For example, if an Influencer or celebrity is planning a day out and wants a good aesthetic atmosphere for her vlog or HXT post, we'll usher a few people in. Set up a good barista behind the counter of the Influencer's "favorite" café. Get some extras to walk up and down the streets to make the city look vibrant. But they're only stage props. Once filming is done, everyone goes back to their homes. The only buildings that have people in them all the time are the factories where all our pretty props are made; the social media centers where people sit behind computers all day, monitoring things; and the Leader's headquarters, where the CEO of HXT lives and governs and has people waiting on her hand and foot."

"This is crazy," the teenage boy with us exclaims as he

whips his neck this way and that to peer at his surroundings. "I mean, like, it doesn't seem *real.*"

"How come it's so… dark?" Ariel asks.

She's got a point, I notice, as I'm silently soaking in everything. The entire world seems to be painted in fuzzy monochromatic tones. The sky is a dim shade of gray, no sun. The buildings are all gray too, and the lifeless windows are stark black on their facades. The streets are plain and colorless, as are the strips of nature you get glimpses of in the distance: small city-adjacent parks, tiny clusters of trees. Nothing like what you see on TV. Could this whole ploy be *that* elaborate? It's almost unbelievable.

"Oh, yeah," Loren snorts. The laugh isn't a mirthful one, it's a harsh, scornful sound. "Forgive me for using the theater analogy over and over, but it's because no one's turned the stage lights on. See, our world isn't a pretty one. It's not glamorous, it's not dreamy. It's exactly what you see right now. Gray. Desolate. At least, until, someone needs to film something. Anytime there is a commercial, a photo shoot, anything — the power is switched on. Everything, literally, comes down to a single switch in the CEO's command room. With one button, she can make a gorgeous yellow sun appear. She can create warmth, or winds, or autumn leaves. She can place people here or there, like figures in a video game. She can inject the trees with color. And not even just a regular, natural green. When the lights are turned on, everything is ultra-vivid. Did you ever play with color sticks as a kid? It's like those. Like everything is painted with those super-pigmented sticks. Perfect for giving the impression of perfection."

I shake my head as I follow behind her clacking heels. My mind is blown and running in so many directions, I can barely keep up with my own thoughts.

"One thing I don't understand," says Elle Doherty, the

first words she's spoken since we landed, "is her agenda. The CEO, I mean. I thought she wanted to create a *genuine* utopia. Why spend all this time and money creating something drab just to lie about it on camera? Why separate us and horde all you kids here like elite cattle? Heck, this world is almost as drab as ours. What's the point of separation?"

Elle has a great point. That realization hits me hard, all of a sudden. What *is* her agenda? And who is she, anyway? Why is she so secretive, so insistent on keeping her identity an enigma? What doesn't she want us to know — apart from the catastrophic truth that the Influencer World isn't the great, happy place we all thought it was.

"I don't know," Loren says with a sigh. She swivels her head around to look at us, at me. "But that's why you have to confront her, isn't it?"

Confront HXT's CEO? I feel a shiver of fear until I realize — she's right. That's what this is about, what it's always been about. The only way we have any hope of taking down their world and restoring hope to ours is to conquer the woman in charge.

Of course, that'll be way easier said than done.

Loren begins to walk faster. She extends an arm and points up ahead.

"Down there is the train station. It never runs, except when someone needs it to. It'll take us to winner's row. Once we're at my house, we can start making plans."

I look at her in awe as we dash the rest of the way toward the train. What is her story? Why is she so blunt with the truth and no one else is? She has more fame and glory than every Influencer on the planet — why doesn't she want to hold onto that with an iron fist?

The train looms ahead, an old, rusty hunk of metal

that looks like it's definitely seen better days. Together, the six of us make a beeline for the platform in front of it.

Well, I guess I'm about to find out.

———

LOREN WAS RIGHT ABOUT THE TRAIN. UP UNTIL SHE PLACED her handprint on a little touchscreen on the side of it, the thing looked like it had been abandoned. But once Loren identifies herself, the train rouses from its slumber, with mechanical rumbles and whines, and it stirs to life. The doors slide open, the lights flicker on, and a cool, feminine voice resonates from unseen speakers, saying, *"Welcome. Please board now."*

I eye the train like it is an alien as I climb inside. Vehicles, even in my world, are technologically advanced, and there are many self-driving cars. But I've never seen a self-driving train.

During the ride, we are given many snacks and drinks by machines built into the compartments.

"Don't eat it," Loren warns when my sister reaches for a cinnamon roll. "It's nothing but cardboard."

Ariel sits back, disappointed. I stare at the food in awe. Everything there looks as real and genuine as the lines on my hand. Take the cinnamon roll, for example. It even *glistens* like the real thing, its sugary glaze and cinnamon swirls worthy of the display case of some fancy bakery. My stomach is still full of the cake from earlier, but I am curious to bite into the cinnamon roll, just for the sake of seeing what a cardboard pastry tasted like.

"What happens if you eat it?" Greg asks, the curly-haired fifteen-year-old bringing up my next question for me.

"Me? Nothing. It will just go through me like it doesn't

exist at all. But if one of *you* eat it… it would be like ingesting a mountain of plastic. You'd probably poison yourself."

I frown at the blonde sitting across from me. "What do you mean by that? Why would you be okay with it? Wouldn't it poison all of us the same?"

Loren doesn't answer that question. Her eyes shift away from me, out the window where new scenery has cropped up. A long stretch of road lined with cherry blossom trees, brick mailboxes, and huge, lofty homes.

"We're here! Winner's Row."

The train comes to a gentle stop, and the automated female voice from before blares out one last time, thanking us for being such good passengers. The six of us rise, but just as we're starting to approach the doors, Loren comes to a sudden halt. Her body tenses up.

"What's wrong?" I ask, immediately concerned, even before the others.

"It's… nothing. I'm just… getting a call from my publicist."

My blood turns to ice. Have they found out about us?

Loren turns away, shielding herself from view. I watch her, concerned and curious at the same time. I can't be sure, but for a moment, when she brushes her hair aside and reaches up with her right hand, it looks like she's pressing on the nape of her neck, like a button is embedded in her skin.

Then she starts talking in a low, soft voice.

"Yeah. Yeah, I just made it. No, no, I'm fine. The others though… right, bloodbath… Oh? Okay, I got it. Yeah, I just got home, so I'll throw something up. Yeah. Bye."

A second later, she turns back around to face us all. "Okay, so, my publicist was saying that the Internet's going nuts because I haven't posted in a while, and everyone thinks I died in the mob at City Hall. So, I'm gonna have to post something, to reassure the fans. Also, you need to let me go out first, just to make sure none of the other Influencers are outside or anything."

We nod quickly, all of us eager to get out of this train and in the safe four walls of Loren's house.

Once she is gone, the Dohertys converge on my sister and I. Rick moves in close, leaning toward me conspiratorially.

"Did anyone else notice that phone call?" he says. "There wasn't actually a *phone* involved."

"Maybe she used one of their hologram thingies," Ariel suggests.

But Elle shakes her head. "Holograms, from what I've seen of them, are huge. We would have seen it."

We all keep quiet, descending into outward silence while our inner monologues have a field day with our chaotic thoughts.

Then Greg speaks up, with the kind of sassy, no-nonsense remark only a person of his age would articulate: "There's some freaky crap going on here."

He's right. I'd imagined this whole thing to be no bigger or more complex than a simple case of a greedy woman doing greedy things. But I've only been in the Influencer World for two seconds, and already, that idea of life over the Wall is crumbling. Things are not that simple here. Something's going on — but what?

Loren comes back quickly. She flings open the doors with an urgency that gives us all whiplash as we make sharp turns to face her.

"Hurry," she whispers. "The coast is clear for now, but Adam Ridley's throwing a birthday party next door —

should be safe, since they're all in the backyard, but you can never be too careful."

An ear-splitting squeal erupts from my little sister's mouth. "You live next to Adam Ridley? Oh, can you please, *please*, introduce us?"

"Ariel!" I scold. "Are you forgetting *nobody*'s supposed to see us?"

Laughing nervously, Loren reaches out to take Ariel's hand and pull her out of the train onto the springy ground below. "Your brother's right," she says. "We all need to stay under the radar as long as we possibly can. Besides, Adam's really not that awesome. He's kind of a jerk actually."

Ariel gasps. Her face collapses.

I once read about the legends of the Old World, in particular the one about the jovial gift-bringing grandfather figure — Santa Claus. I read that kids used to truly believe the Christmas icon existed — many were heartbroken when their parents revealed the truth.

That's how my little sister looks now. Like her hero's just been declared a figment of imagination. I realize Ariel must be going through a lot right now. She's idolized the Influencer World and the people in it for nearly a decade now. What must it feel like to finally come here and realize it was all a lie?

Once we're all out of the train, Loren leads the way down the neighborhood street.

The scenery of Winner's Row blows my mind. Though it's just like the city center — fancy, but dark — the street is one of the wealthiest I've ever seen. The homes themselves look like they'd cost more than me, my parents, and their parents before them ever earned in our entire lifetimes. They sit like kings and queens clothed in brick, marble, and stucco on pristinely trimmed pieces of green lawn.

Each of the sixty houses on that long, winding street are at least four stories high, with flowered bushes, lofty stone pillars, and elaborate water fountains adorning the exterior.

Loren takes us to a palace made of white marble. It has an extra story, and stands taller than all the other mansions. The yard is bigger too, with enough room for a rose garden alongside the fountain. If this whole street was full of government officials, the giant marble palace would be the President's home, while the others would belong to powerful senators and politicians.

This place is none other than Loren Harper's home.

"Why is your house the fanciest?" Greg asks as we are hurrying up her cobblestone driveway.

"It wasn't always," she says. "When I first won the tournament, I had a regular house like all the others here. But when I became… well, what I am now…"

"The CEO's number one moneymaker, you mean?" I put forth.

"Yeah. When I reached that level of fame, they redid the house."

"I guess there are perks to being the nation's It Girl," Greg says. "This house is awesome!"

"It's lonely," Loren says quietly.

It seems I'm the only one who hears or notices the vulnerable response.

Then she throws open her huge double doors and leads us into the crystalline entrance hall beyond.

Chapter 11

Almost as soon as we're inside, Loren runs off, dashing up the massive spiral staircase with a hastily thrown command over her shoulder: *Make yourselves at home.*

Briefly, I wonder what she's up to. But then the grandeur of the place takes my breath away, and shifts my attention. My head swivels this way and that, moving so fast I almost give myself whiplash. But there is so much to see in every direction. The giant living room opening out to my left. The collection of intricate oil paintings lining the corridor walls on my right. The gleaming marble floors that are so smooth and shiny they look like water. The pillars, the high arched ceilings, the giant chandelier. It's so extravagant, unlike anything I've ever seen before, even in the movies.

But I find myself wondering if any of it's real. If the fancy furniture isn't just made of well-designed and highly-decorated cardboard. If the floors beneath my feet are really just plastic made to look and feel like high quality stone.

All five of us are so entranced, we never even leave our spots, rooted to the floor in the entrance hall. We just stand there for a good five minutes, gaping at everything.

Then Loren comes click-clacking down the stairs. She changed while she was up there. Now, her young and vulnerable face looks older beneath all the extra makeup she's put on to darken her eyes and widen her lips. Instead of the dress she wore to the ceremony, she's in a pair of high-waisted shorts and a shirt that is cropped short to show off a bare strip of her tan, flat stomach. Her golden hair is the same, except now she has straightened out the waves with a flat iron. Now she looks more like the girl you see everywhere on television and the Internet. She looks less like a person, more like one of them.

She carries her phone and a selfie stick as she hurries down the stairs back into our midst.

"I have to go drop in at Adam's party," she says. "Take a few pictures, post a few videos. Shouldn't take me long. Make yourselves comfortable."

With that, she flies through the front doors and disappears within seconds, leaving only a faintly sweet perfume smell behind.

That is the trigger that sets us all in motion.

The Dohertys immediately hurry off, all three of them branching away in separate directions. Elle seems to be making a beeline for the kitchen, Rick is veering right toward an open space that looks like a fancy sitting room, and Greg is sprinting up the staircase like a little kid.

Leaving just Ariel and me.

I look at her. Give her a small smile. "So… any place you'd like to look at first?"

"Yeah," she says.

The tiny twist of her mouth is strangely guilty, and a

second after peering into her eyes, I know what her answer is.

I sigh. "You want to eavesdrop on the party next door, don't you?"

Ariel blushes. "Well, I mean… it's *Adam Ridley.* And all the other Influencers. I mean, aren't *you* curious? If everything else in this world is fake, then…"

Then the party has to be fake, too. She has a point.

"Okay, you've convinced me. Let's see if we can find a window."

For the next few minutes, Ariel and I journey through the massive house, which seems to get bigger the further we went in. There are a multitude of shiny glass panes on the ground floor, but those windows are too low to provide much of a vantage point. So, we explore the second and third floors, before finally finding a window on the fourth-floor landing.

It is a tall cut of glass that nearly takes up the entire West Wall, and overlooks the side of Loren's yard, and beyond: the neighbor's backyard, where Adam Ridley's party is in full swing.

"It… *looks* like a party," Ariel says, shock in her voice.

My sister is right. For a moment, the festivities next door *do* look genuine. There are snack tables set up and plush patio furniture in a corner, and a dozen gorgeously made-up people dancing, laughing, chatting, and videoing themselves in the middle of the green yard. There is music and loud voices that carry, even all the way to this window.But… something isn't right.

Something isn't… *normal.*

It's too staged. It reminds me of a play, an extremely well-done theater production. Everyone there, in their glittery costumes, has a role. The wild dancers, the beautiful gigglers, the talkative social butterflies. And, of course, the birthday boy himself, Adam Ridley, who makes his way around the crowd, popping in on people's selfies and videos, saying hi and dishing out hugs like they're going out of style. It looks like every party scene in a movie.

Too real. Real enough to be fake.

"Is it just me or… is something about this… creepy?" Ariel asks.

I nod. "Yes. Very creepy."

We stand frozen in front of the window, watching the landscape below us.

And then — all of a sudden — the festivities stop.

The music cuts off. The selfie sticks lower, the voices quiet. Cameras are switched off, and smiles are wiped away with somber expressions.

The ground rumbles, and all the Influencers scatter, running to the edges of the yard to keep the middle of it open. And there, in the center of the grass, the rumble is the loudest. It sounds like an earthquake, but strangely mechanical. Ariel and I are all but pressing our noses to the window, unable to look away.

But a second later, I wish I could look away. I wish we both could unsee everything.

A gleaming glass cylinder pokes at the grass like a zombie reaching its decayed hand up through its grave. With a gasp, my sister latches onto my shoulders, throwing herself at me like she's five years old again, scared of a shadow in her closet. There is a droning hum as the cylinder pushes itself up slowly, like an elevator, from somewhere underground. When it finally stops moving, the woman trapped inside slides aside the front glass pane and steps out into the yard.

She moves weird, like there's a problem with her joints, and when she speaks, the voice that comes out of her reminds me of the artificial intelligence robots that are built into homes of the wealthy, programs like Amelia and Sera that are supposed to make lives easier.

"That was good," she says, speaking to the crowd of Influencers while her eyes stay glued to the tablet in her hands. "Except for you, Wendy. Comments point out fatigue, lazy dancing, tired eyes. Weakness must not be shown."

The girl named Wendy steps forward, her face gloomy. She has blazing red hair and a small, petite figure barely covered in her skimpy party dress. She looks like the kind of girl people describe as a spitfire, but right then, she looks like she's going to faint from exhaustion.

She starts talking, but her voice is too low. It doesn't reach us.

Before I can stop her, my sister takes it upon herself to push the window open. I hiss at her, but she doesn't listen. Thankfully, none of the people down below seem to notice. The redhead's voice floats up with as much loudness and clarity as if she stood in the same room as us.

"… not charged in a while," she is saying. "I'm… exhausted."

The woman with the tablet lifts her head and gives Wendy a pinched, disapproving look.

But then another Influencer steps forward. A boy with platinum blonde hair.

"We're *all* tired," he says with a sigh.

The woman purses her lips. "Very well. Ten-minute charging for all of you. But after that, the party must be in full swing, bigger, better, flashier than ever."

A murmur of agreement runs through the crowd, and then the robotic woman steps back into her weird glass tube and is lowered back down into the Earth. Once she is gone, and the machine-hum over, the grass smoothes over of its own accord. It looks exactly like it did five minutes ago.

But the Influencers don't.

They all hang their heads, flopping their bodies over and folding in on themselves, like they're asleep standing up.

And maybe they are. Their eyes are closed. They *could* be sleeping, but…

All of them? At the exact same second? Moving the exact same way?

And there's no snoring, no breathing. They're completely still, limp and lifeless, yet stiff at the same time, like dolls who have been bent at the waist by their owners.

The strangest thing is, the mechanical hum is still in the air. Even though the underground elevator is long gone.

"Oh, my gosh," Ariel gasps.

Footsteps sound on the floor behind us, but we don't turn.

"What's going on here?" a voice asks.

"What are you guys looking at?"

Ariel and I are paralyzed. We just stand and stare and hold our breaths.

The Doherty family converges on us, rushing to our sides and crowding around the window to see what we're seeing. It only takes a second for all three of their faces to pale, drained of all color. Then they're as frozen and silent as we are.

Greg is the first to speak up, to release the haunted words none of us are brave enough to articulate out loud.

"They're… robots," he says.

Chapter 12

en minutes seem to last ten hours.

Then at last, all at the same time, the Influencers begin to stir. They straighten up, lifting their heads and opening their eyes with the same, identical motion. The hum dissipates from the air, leaving only a loud, empty silence. Their charging session over now, they resume the party. Music returns, seemingly louder than ever after the thick silence. Phones and cameras are whipped out again. Influencers film themselves and the others around them, their voices high with exaggerated happiness, their faces bright with plastic joy.

In the midst of all the mayhem, Loren stands out. She's not joining in on the festivities — instead, she walks to the edge of the yard toward Adam Ridley. Something stirs within me when I watch them embrace. She says a few words to him, which he takes with a warm smile and a nod before watching her leave.

"Quick, she's coming back," Greg announces, as if that isn't obvious by her swift-footed stride off the property and back toward her own. "What are we gonna do? Should we confront her? Ask her about all that weirdness?"

"Oh, definitely not," Ariel and Elle say at the same time.

But Rick and I are of a different mind.

"We need to find out the truth," I say. "How are we gonna survive this, otherwise?"

"Geez." Rick sighs and runs a hand through his thinning hair. "I never imagined we'd be dealing with *robots*. This is nuts, absolutely nuts. I mean, *none* of them are real. Can you believe that?"

"No," I say. I'm already inching toward the staircase. "But it doesn't matter. Loren will be here any second. Let's go."

At that, we all hurry down the stairs, a cluster of five frantic humans on their way to face one mechanical person.

We reach the front foyer just as Loren is opening the door. She sweeps in, gives the five of us a relieved smile, and then quickly drops the expression once she sees our faces.

"What's wrong?" she asks. "Did... did someone see you?"

Ariel and the Dohertys all turn their heads to look at me. Somehow, during the course of all this chaos, I've become the main man in this bizarre equation. I'm the one everyone is staring pointedly at to make the next move.

So, with a sigh, I take a step forward, cross my arms, and tell Loren, "No. But *we* saw *you*."

At first, she frowns. I study her face, trying to find anything fake or mechanic there. But these robots are *good*. There is absolutely no indication that the girl before me isn't entirely human.

Except, of course, for all the signs that came before this moment.

The strange metal-ringing sound it made when Loren fell down at City Hall.

The way none of them eat.

The bizarre button she pressed to take a phone call from her publicist — the button that was *embedded* in her skin.

All the signs were there. Now, I'm reading them.

In a second, her expression changes. She *knows*.

"Oh," she says.

"Yeah, what the heck was that all about?" Greg asks, tactless.

Her eyes stay focused on mine. They don't even flit in his direction as she answers, in a quiet voice, "We were charging."

For some reason, anger boils inside me. My reply is snippy and cynical. "What, technology is not advanced enough to make robots run endlessly?"

Guilt springs up at the sight of her expression, but I push it down and turn away from her. Stalking off down the hall, I find the first room with a couch in it and take refuge there. My thoughts are a whirlwind. Why did she look so wounded when I made that comment? She's a robot. She's *fake*. She shouldn't be able to feel any emotion beyond what they tell her to feel for publicity's sake.

At least the couch beneath me seems real enough, not cardboard.

A minute passes, and then footsteps sound. The smell of floral perfume reaches me before she does, and I stiffen. I'm trying to cool down here. The last person I need to see right now is Loren.

But she sweeps into the room, nonetheless. Ignoring

my glare, she parks herself on the couch beside me, but not too close.

"Why are you so upset?" she asks. "I mean, you know that this whole world is fake."

"Yeah, but I didn't know the *people* in it were, too," I growl. "I mean, can you imagine how jarring it is to find out the girl you're falling for really isn't a girl at all, but a… a machine? A jumble of wires and technology?"

Loren doesn't say anything. A moment too late, I realize I've said way too much.

Before the awkwardness can spiral out of control, I quickly change the subject.

"Why is she doing this, anyway? I mean, it's her, isn't it? The CEO?"

"Yes."

"Well, what's up with that? Why does she feel the need to turn you all into freaking robots? And how is she doing it? I mean, are you partially still human? Did she… did she *kill* you…?"

Loren sighs and stands up. "It's a long story. We'd be better off figuring out a plan to defeat her."

"We will." I stand up to join her. "But I need to know all the back story before I can move forward. I need to know what I'm up against. Just… give me the abridged version."

She cracks a tiny smile, but it never spreads into something more. In fact, it fades quickly, and a somber expression takes over. She faces away from me as she says, "Being an Influencer is not all it's cracked up to be. In fact, that's the first thing people find out when they come over the Wall for the first time. It's *depressing.* I mean, the constant pressure to post and be active online is hard enough. But then, you find out everything they show you on TV is a lie. Our world is nothing but illusions. We don't even get to eat. I'm not surprised the people here don't make it. I'd be shocked if they did. But that's why she has to make us into robots. We *are* all dead. But that's not something she did. Or maybe she did, inadvertently. But we killed ourselves because we couldn't bear this place."

I suck in a sharp breath. Not only am I falling for a machine, but I'm falling for a corpse turned into a machine?

"So, what, does the CEO just pull everyone up from their graves?"

Loren shakes her head. "No, we're still in the ground. Sort of. Well, she takes our brains. That's how we're able to... to think and feel. But the rest of us is just a bioengineered shell. She uses our DNA to create exact replicas of our bodies, our voices. She steals our faces. Everything is attached to a perfectly designed automaton. We are not like the old-world robots. We're even created to be *soft*. See?"

She swoops in close to me before I even have time to brace myself and reaches for my hand. I hold my breath as the lightness of her palm touches mine. Her skin is *warm*. If I hadn't seen the truth for myself, I'd laugh if you told me this girl is a robot.

"Wow…" I sigh in awe, staring at our clasped hands.

Then she releases me just as quickly as she grabbed me, and turns away again.

"Anyway," she says. "That's the abridged version. What happens next?"

"Well…" I sniff, and try to regain my focus, but there's a pleasant, fluttery fog in my brain that makes it hard to think. "Um… well, first of all, I guess we need to plan our ambush. Do you know where the CEO lives? Do you know how to get there?"

Loren nods. "Her mansion isn't far from here. All the Influencers have to go there when they first arrive."

"Why?"

"To have 'dinner' with her." Loren makes air quotes with her finger, an extremely human gesture that baffles me. "But no actual eating happens. It's just a glorified meeting where she tells you all the rules and takes your DNA for her robots, should you ever commit suicide."

I balk at the idea, but nod quickly. There's no time to waste freaking out over the CEO's malicious practices.

"Okay," I say. "So, maybe that's how we could get in. By pretending we're the tournament winner, coming for our 'dinner' party."

Loren shakes her head, wincing. "The CEO is all over the Internet. She knows everything that's going on. She'll have already figured out that Jeena is dead, and that no new Influencers are coming."

Something prickly makes my skin crawl. "If she knows everything…"

But Loren shakes her head vehemently, shutting down that fear before I even have time to voice it. "Don't worry. She's not all-knowing. She just spends all day in her control room. It's this gigantic chamber filled with a million computers, with every computer showing a different corner of the Internet. She knows stuff, but only what is portrayed online. And trust me — we weren't seen. I made sure of it."

I nod again, then frown at her. I really should drop the issue. After all, it's not entirely pertinent to our current mission. But it lodges itself in my throat like a bite of food that won't go down. I have to get it out.

"Loren," I say, "what's the deal with you? If you're a robot like everyone else, how come you've developed feelings, and the others haven't?"

Her big green eyes flicker to mine. "Oh, we all have feelings. We all want out. I'm just the only one willing to do something about it. I'm the only one who had to watch this horrible world drain my parents and take their life away. The others have been wrapped up in fame too long. Their online platform is the only thing that keeps them going. Me, I've never cared that much about being an Influencer. I only joined the tournament ten years ago to save my family from poverty. I thought… I thought life over the Wall would be better for us."

The lump in my throat returns at the sight of her glistening eyes. I try to distract her from her pain by changing the subject.

"So, you're saying, deep down, all the other Influencers feel the same way as you do? They're just too scared to give up their fame and do something about it?"

Loren nods sadly. "It's really a tragedy, isn't it? We're all trapped in this hell. We can't even get relief from dying, because we never really cease to exist — our brains and memories are forced to live on forever in the body of a machine."

I sigh and roll my eyes up toward the vaulted ceiling above me. Anger rampages through me like a wildfire bent on destroying everything in its path. I don't know how I'm going to defeat HXT's CEO, but right now, killing her with my bare hands is the most appealing plan of action.

Chapter 13

Soon after that, we round up the others. At first, we think we have to explain everything for Ariel, Greg, Elle, and Rick, but turns out, they were eavesdropping on our conversation the whole time. They already know, and they're already prepared. Not needing to waste time there, we launch right into our strategy.

"Okay, here's what you need to know," Loren explains to us. "The CEO is gripped mainly by greed. The whole reason she keeps this whole scheme up is to continue enticing new Influencers over the Wall. More Influencers equal more cash streams. It's all about money with her. But she also has a problem with death. This is something I've sort of deduced on my own. She wants to be immortal, see. To live forever with her billions. And she's done it. Killing her will be impossible, just as it's impossible to permanently destroy us. If you think our robot technology is advanced, you should see *hers.*"

"Whoa, whoa, wait a second." Greg Doherty lifts one hand and two eyebrows. "You're saying that woman's a robot, too?"

Loren nods like it's nothing. "Of course. Where do you think she got the idea? She was her own guinea pig, in the beginning. She started playing around with robotics and cloning and a whole bunch of other science-y, tech stuff I don't understand. Long before the Wall was even built. She created herself as the prototype robot, and when it worked, she came up with the genius idea to do it to a million other people. She pitched the idea to doctors, claimed it would erase illness and prolong life. But they all laughed at her and said she was nuts. So, she went a different direction. She saw that the world was quickly being taken over by social media and Internet celebrities, so she hopped on the bandwagon with the plan to combine her two loves — money and immortality. The rest is simple: she created a fake, beautiful world, constructed a wall to make the fake world look elitist and appealing, and the outside world dull and depressing. Then she started pooling in her Influencers. When they all started killing themselves, she shoved them into bots. Then she started the tournament to bring in more and more Influencers. The cycle never ends. And it never *will* end, unless we do something about it."

Every one of our jaws drop to the floor. For a long moment, we're dumbstruck. Speechless. None of us ever imagined the sprawling Wall and the world beyond it could be traced down to one woman's greed and her mad scientist dreams. I always knew the CEO gave me a bad feeling, and now, I know why.

"Alright, so what is the plan?" Rick asks. "If she's impossible to kill, how will we put a stop to this madness?"

This question silences us all. Rick has a point. If violence won't work, what will?

To my surprise, it's my little sister who comes up with the most brilliant suggestion. "Why don't we do an exposé and leak it all over the Internet?"

"What?" Loren frowns, looking at Ariel like she's nuts.

And she's not the only one. I can tell by the expressions on all the faces around me that they're quickly dismissing her idea. Even I am confused for a minute, until she explains.

"Think about it," she says, splaying her hands, imploring us with her dark brown eyes. "The whole reason the CEO's world continues to go on is because of fans, because followers continue to buy into the propaganda and are endlessly enamored with their Influencer idols. But if suddenly, they *weren't* anymore, think about the domino effect that would have. If everyone online is suddenly disillusioned with life over the Wall, that frees up the Influencers to stop torturing themselves for fame's sake. We could convince them to join us, and you know what they say about strength in numbers and all that. If enough of us banded together, we might have a shot at overthrowing the CEO."

One by one, each of us start to smile. Her idea is so clever, it's almost shocking. Why didn't we think of it? I can see the question dawn in everyone's eyes. A second ago, they were glaring at my sister like she was a dumb, silly teenager. Now, they're gazing with wonder at her.

"Amazing!" Rick exclaims. "That's awesome! Don't kill the CEO herself, kill her pride and joy. That'll destroy her for sure."

"But we can't," Loren says, her face pinched. "Don't you remember what I said about her monitoring everything we do online? She's constantly checking up on what the Influencers are posting. If she sees something like that, she'll instantly take it down."

"Not if it's live," I say, grinning as the plan forms in my head. "If we do it as a live stream, she'll have no way of stopping the words coming out of your mouth in real time.

She might be able to erase it afterwards, but by then, already the entire world will have seen it. *Everyone* and their dog watches your live videos."

Loren shakes her head, but I can see the idea taking root in her mind. She's almost there, almost to the point of agreeing, yet still searching for a reason not to.

"It won't work," she says. "She'll do anything to stop me, cut off my phone, drop the connection."

"How about we do it from one of our phones?" Ariel suggests. "She might still be able to shut it off, but it'll buy us some time if you're connected to a separate device. You've just gotta get it all out quickly, or at least most of it. Enough to send the Internet into a frenzy."

Loren sighs. She takes a deep breath, then sighs it out again. Her eyes are wary, but determined, too.

"Alright," she finally says. "I'll do it."

She's brave, I realize as I watch her position herself on the edge of the couch, straightening her spine and lifting her chin. The other Influencers aren't simply cowards — they're *normal.* Wouldn't we all, if faced with what they were facing, rather keep quiet and take what feeble excuse for life we could get rather than stir the pot and risk rejection?

Not Loren Harper. Loren is courageous. She has *heart.*

Once she is posed just right, I fix my phone to a tripod and position it in front of her, so she's in the center of the camera's focus. The others crowd around me, standing just out of sight but with a perfect view of the girl who's about to shake the entire world.

She's given me her account information, so I log into

her HXT account from my phone, and then bring up the live stream page. Her face pops up on the screen, glowing, without a hint of anxiety.

My finger hovers over the record button. "You ready?"

The robot girl on the couch gives a cheesy human answer. "As ready as I'll ever be."

And then I press the button. There is a red flash. We're officially live, broadcasting to every living person in the entire world.

Within a half-second, the little bar at the bottom shows ten billion viewers, one million comments and counting, and triple the amount of likes. My stomach tenses up. Already, she's got the entire planet's attention. There's no telling what kind of nationwide, catastrophic mayhem is about to take place.

Loren takes a deep breath. In the time it takes her to exhale it, twenty million more people start viewing the stream.

Then she officially starts with one line, "Hey, I'm Loren Harper, and today's live is gonna be a little different."

The next five minutes are the most intense of my life. The tension in the air is so real I swear I can reach out and touch it. Loren speaks fast, faster than I thought possible, and somehow manages to get out most of what she told me. With bated breath and pounding hearts, our group of five watches her go through all the ugly truths of the Influencer World, starting with the fakeness of it all. She even proves she's a robot by turning slightly and showing the camera a slit in the skin on the back of her neck. This she pulls slightly, revealing an opening that exposes all the metal and wires inside her. The moment's kind of gross, but a stark realization. Nobody will doubt what she's saying now.

For the first time since she's started talking, I take my eyes off her and look at the phone. The comments section is blowing up. Everyone is reeling, and that shows through the capital letters and exclamation points they send firing like missiles. Horror bleeds through their words, but also sympathy. And — surprisingly — *guilt*. People are actually voicing shame at falling for the scheme and perpetuating it, for fueling the CEO's greed and evil plans.

And not only that, but they're voicing *revenge*.

It's even more intense than I imagined. They don't just feel sorry for Loren; they're planning to raise Hell for her sake. But I'm not surprised, not really. She *is* the most loved girl in the entire world. That's why she is the perfect candidate for this.

But once she creeps toward ten minutes, it's clear the CEO has found out and is now doing everything in her power to stop her.

The lights flicker on and off.

Loren cries out and grasps at her body, as if the wires inside her are malfunctioning, causing her pain.

The connection wavers, and as my phone is attacked, the camera turns fuzzy, sending Loren's face out of focus. But for the moment, the Internet is still intact, and I'm able to see what people are saying in the comments.

They're freaking out, mostly.

But a common thread is running through the conversation.

People are planning to avenge Loren, just as we'd hoped they would.

Everyone, from now on, let's boycott HXT and all the Influencers!

Don't worry, Loren, we'll try our best to end this!!!

Can't believe that awful man did this to you...officially boycotting.

Let's all camp out at our various corners of the Wall. Maybe if enough of us try, we can go over and try to rescue Loren.

But then — it happens. Finally, the CEO is able to shut my phone off. The live stream ends; my phone screen turns black.

Loren lifts her head. Her eyes are wide with terror. "She's going to kill me."

Panic flares in my chest. I fly like a bullet to her side. "Why do you say that?"

"Because she just told me. Through my chip."

I've never been more afraid in my life, but I suppress the feeling and make myself calm for her sake. With my arm around her shoulders, I say, "Okay, but don't worry. You didn't see the comments, Loren. Literally *everyone* said they're going to fight for you. Our plan is working."

Loren's eyes swim with tears. She shakes her head, then flings her arms around my neck. Despite the fact that her skin isn't real, it is the warmest, softest hug I've ever felt. Her grip is strong, yet timid. And when she pulls away, terror strikes me.

Her eyes have glazed over. And as I watch, in real time, they fix on mine before slowly falling shut. She slumps over on the couch, and when I touch her, she is ice-cold.

"How… how did she *do* that?" While I am rendered motionless, speechless, Ariel voices this question. Her throat wobbles, and I know she is about to cry, if the tears haven't escaped already.

"She's a robot," I say, swallowing hard. "All she'd have to do is press a button."

I feel just as close to breaking down as my sister is, but I pull myself together. It's weird that my heart is breaking so much for a girl I barely knew, let alone one who isn't even real, but I don't deny the intensity of it. Still, I can't cry.

Not yet. This thing is far from over, and I have to be strong for Loren.

"Alright," I say firmly, rising to face the four white-faced people in front of me. "If we're gonna do this, we have to do it now."

"Do what?" Ariel whimpers.

"We have to destroy the CEO," I say. "Now, I don't know where her house is, but Loren said it wasn't far from here. We need to find it, sneak in, and kill her."

"How though?" Rick asks. "I mean, Harper already said the woman was virtually indestructible."

I wave my hand at the cold robot lying on the couch. "Did you not just see what happened? She *died*. Somehow, the CEO was able to kill her, most likely with a button in her command room that corresponds to her system. Now tell me this — if the CEO experimented on herself before turning half the Earth into bots, how do you think she invented the instant-kill feature if she didn't first discover the technology for her own self?"

Everyone's eyes widen. They look even more shocked now than when Loren died.

"You're right!" Elle gasps. "There *is* a way to kill her!"

"I bet she has a whole dashboard dedicated to her own robot self," I say, the theories flying out of my mouth as soon as they pop up in my head. "She probably keeps it under lock and key, but I guarantee you, it's there. If we can detain her long enough, and somehow manage to infiltrate her command center, I'm sure we could take over her system. And from there, it would only be as simple as pushing a button. Just like with Loren."

The Dohertys start nodding. So does my sister. I can see it on their faces — the plan is taking shape in their minds, becoming clearer. We can actually do this. We actually have a chance here.

"But wait," Rick says, instantly stabbing everyone's excitement balloons, "how are we gonna do all this if we don't even know how to get to her place?"

Before I even have time to answer, the doorbell rings.

<h1 style="text-align:center">Chapter 14</h1>

$\mathcal{W}$e all jump.

Fear penetrates the room, thick and impossible to see through, like coils of early morning fog.

"Who the heck is that?" Greg Doherty exclaims.

With the most frightened expression I've ever seen on her face, my little sister says, "What if it's *her*? Or one of her guards, coming to kill us? I mean, I'm sure she knows we're here. Loren using your phone probably tipped her off."

"Oh, she'll want to destroy us, I'm sure," I say. "But I guarantee you her focus is elsewhere at the moment."

"Where?"

I shrug. "Damage control, of course. The Internet's going crazy right now. She can see her empire's on the verge of collapse. She and her team are probably doing everything they can to rectify the situation, to change people's minds and get them back on board with the Influencer thing. She'll start worrying about us later — probably once she realizes that nobody is going to change their minds. Not now, after what they've seen."

"But then… if not the CEO or one of her bot employees… who else could it be?"

To Greg's question, I merely sigh, square my shoulders, and start for the doorway. "The only way to find out is to go downstairs and see."

The others seem reluctant, but they fall into step with me, anyway. It's not confidence I'm feeling as I walk downstairs — more like a certain complacence. I've already resigned myself to whatever fate awaits me. I will try my best to destroy the CEO once and for all, but even if I end up dying first, I am confident in the rest of the world. I have no doubt that they'll be doing everything they can to avenge Earth's sweetheart — if I can't destroy the Influencer World, it will only be a matter of time before everyone else does.

The doorbell rings a second time, just when the five of us have reached the foyer. I am the one up front, the one who reaches out first and grasps the doorknob, giving it a sharp twist.

When the door opens, I am shocked to see who is standing on the other side.

A horde of at least a hundred people are there. They are all beautiful, made up, and glamorous. Guys and girls alike. They are all Influencers.

"Um… hello," I say, awkwardly. "What are you all doing here?"

The guy at the front of the group is Adam Ridley.

He wears a steely, determined expression, despite the childish party hat still stuck on his head.

"We saw Loren's live stream," he says, "and we're ready to fight now. Loren freed us all — we've been wanting to revolt against this place for ages. Now, we can. You'll let us join you, won't you?"

Ariel, Greg, Elle, and Rick all break out into reckless smiles.

But there's one thing I have to know before I accept Adam's proposal.

"Do you guys know how to get to the CEO's house?"

The Influencers start grinning.

Adam says, "Like the back of my hand."

I nod. "Alright, you're in. Let's do this."

———

I NEVER EXPECTED THE INFLUENCERS TO JOIN US SO quickly, but now that they're on our side, the plan falls into place easily.

The first thing we do is head to the train station. While we ride toward the outskirts of the Capitol, where the CEO lives, we keep our eyes on our phones, studying the Internet climate. The entire world is still angry and vengeful, which is good.

A new hashtag has cropped up: *#RevoltForLorenHarper.* Using this, people post pictures of themselves camping out in front of the Wall. Many of them carry dangerous objects — a torch, a sledgehammer, a gun — anything that could help them bring the barrier down. The Influencers around me take time to like everyone's pictures, egging the people on. It's exciting to see people in France, West Virginia, Barbados, Vietnam, and everywhere else, all gathering around their ends of the Earth-spanning border.

It's also humbling. This is not because of anything I've done — this is all Loren. It's crazy how much social media has infiltrated our lives, how the Influencers have taken over literally the entire world, but it's our reality, and I'm going to take advantage of it.

When the train stops, we don't immediately get off.

Adam Ridley stands up and says, "Alright, guys. We need to focus on getting the CEO out of her command room. If we can do that, we can deactivate her robot guards. But we have to do it quickly — the moment she realizes we're in on it, she'll destroy us like she did to Loren."

It becomes clear to me that the robots need to stay out of this — at least, out of the initial phase. So, it's up to me, Ariel, and the Dohertys.

"Alright," I say. "We'll be in charge of luring the CEO out of her room."

"But how are we gonna do that without alerting the guards?" my sister asks. "They can still hurt us, even if we're not robots."

Another Influencer, the spunky redhead, says, "If you guys split up, you might be able to confuse the guards. See, there are various entrances, a guard at each one. If you can make a big enough ruckus at one of the entrances, a few of the guards might leave their posts to come see what's going on, and then we can slip in that way."

"I'll do it," the youngest Doherty says with a sneaky grin on his face. "I'm brilliant at making ruckuses."

"I'll go with him," Ariel says, throwing Greg a sheepish glance.

I refrain from rolling my eyes. Even in a matter of life and death, my little sister has room in her attention for a schoolgirl crush.

"Alright, but be careful," I say, throwing Greg a narrow-eyed look that says, *Take care of my sister, or else.*

Adam starts assigning jobs again. "Me, you, and Wendy" — he points to the redhead — "will swoop in once the coast is clear. I'm not sure where to find her command room, but I have a hunch that it's in the basement. All the top-secret technological stuff is underground."

"That why that lady came out of the hole in the grass at your party?" I ask.

Adam looks surprised to find out I saw that, but nods. "Yeah. Anyway, we'll be in charge of that. And the rest of you guys can camp out around the building, surround it in case she tries to escape."

The Influencers nod.

Then Adam opens the train doors, and all of us crowd out onto the ground outside. We stand at the edge of a lush green valley, sloping upward to a giant hill, at the top of which stands a house even grander and fancier than the palaces on Winner's Row.

The Earth beneath my feet, I notice, feels a lot like that of my hometown.

"This grass feels real," I say.

"It is," Adam confirms. "This is *her* world — she's entitled to all the luxuries."

With that, we start up the hill, which is no problem for the robots, but soon has me and the others out of breath with sore legs.

When we reach the top of the hill, we pause to take inventory of the building before us. It's *massive*, so huge it looks like a giant monster bent on swallowing us up. But the Influencers just look at it with contempt-laced familiarity.

Adam says, "Greg and Ariel — you take the front doors. Rick and Elle, you take the west entrance. We'll head for the back."

Nods all around.

Then we split up.

I stare longingly at my sister as we part ways, hoping she'll be alright. Then I follow Adam and Wendy as they dart in an easterly direction, swerving around the right side of the house and scrambling toward the backyard. But we pause abruptly before we reach it. There, right at the edge of our vision, we catch the outline of a robot guard standing there, back facing us. My heart whams in my chest. I'm so terrified I could scream, but he doesn't notice us. So, we hover there and keep quiet, waiting for the signal.

It only takes a few seconds — then it comes in the form of a crash.

It literally sounds like Greg and Ariel broke the doors down. Shouts ring through the air — followed by a blaring siren that echoes around the mountaintop.

Then there is a second crash — more shouts — probably Rick and Elle's diversion this time.

A second later, a mechanic voice calls out over the shrill alarm, *"BACKUP IS NEEDED, BACKUP IS NEEDED. ALL PERSONNEL REPORT TO THE FRONT AND WEST ENTRANCES."*

The plan works flawlessly.

A second later, the guard in front of us darts inside and hurries away, leaving the entrance wide open.

We creep forward, slowly at first. Then, when we peek around the corner and find the space totally empty, we break out into a run. I hurry behind Adam and Wendy as the throw themselves over the unguarded threshold into the space beyond. Looks like some kind of fancy dining room, but there's no time to analyze anything. For the moment, we're unseen, but I don't count on it lasting long.

Screams, sirens, and scuffling sounds envelop us. I'm tempted to look, to search for Ariel in the mayhem, as we run around, flinging doors open, searching for a set of stairs leading downward. But I refrain. I'm just gonna have to trust that she's alright.

"Over here!" Adam shouts.

His voice nearly gets lost in the other panicky sounds surrounding me, but I manage to hear him just in time. Whirling around, I spot him over by the grand staircase in the entrance hall, which is empty for a split second.

The basement stairs are hidden behind the main stairs. Adam has already flung open the door. I spot a silhouette nearby, but I ignore it and run fast, clearing the distance in two seconds. Wendy is already there with Adam; she grabs my arm, tugs me inside the door, and then the three of us are plunged into silent darkness, shivering in a cluster at the edge of the top step.

Here, the air is pitch black. There is only a cool, blue glow at the bottom of the stairs, but no indication of what lies beyond it.

"Okay, what now?" I hiss at Adam.

"You get down there first," he says. "And distract her, threaten her, whatever. Then we'll sneak in and do whatever damage we can to the operating systems."

I nod and immediately start down the steps. I move fast to give myself zero time for fear. When I reach the bottom, I peer around the corner and see her for the first time.

The chamber is large, the size of three or four living rooms, with every available space taken up by a computer screen. Loren was right — there are *millions*.

And there is someone in the midst of it, though I can hardly call her a woman or a person. She sits in a chair in front of the computers, just staring up at the screens, watching as the Internet breaks down with the truth of her schemes.

But what is she? She looks like a combination of a mannequin, a skeleton, and an alien. She is pasty white, naked, but has no body parts. At least, no human ones. All of her wires and buttons are exposed. She looks like an unfinished doll, or a creature straight from the depths of someone's nightmares. The sight of her fills me with fear, and a desire to vomit at the same time.

But instead of puking, I step around the corner onto the main floor of her dungeon and say, "So, this is why you stay out of the public's eye. I don't blame you."

The chair swivels, and the CEO sees me for the first time. Her eyes are freaky — just two black, glass pebbles set into bizarre indentations. Her mouth, a thin black line that seems to be made of wire, stretches.

"Zachary Eckert," she says. "Age: 27. Occupation: selfie stick assembler. Family: Ariel Eckert, *almost*-winner of the Sixtieth Annual Influencer Tournament. The boy whose phone was used to throw my whole world into disarray. I've been expecting you."

I'm a little freaked out that she has figured out all that just from a single glance, but I don't waste time being afraid.

"I've been expecting you, too," I say. "Your gig is up. The Internet hates you and what you've created. You might as well give up now."

"Give up?" the CEO makes a weird sound, a high-pitched whine that I think she means to be a laugh. Then she adds, "Why would I give up when I'm on the culmination of my newest, greatest technology?"

"Huh?" I frown.

Her wire-mouth stretches wider. "Oh, yes, Zachary. See, this has all worked out in my favor. I've been waiting for the right time to try it and now… well, this is the perfect opportunity."

"Try what?" I ask, narrowing my eyes at her.

My heart beats faster. I'm starting to sweat, to worry. When are Adam and Wendy going to come in here and help me?

"This," says the robot woman.

That is the last thing she says. That is the last thing I hear.

She presses a button on her dashboard, and the whole world goes black.

———

My eyes open. I am stiff, my whole body hard and taut, but I don't mind.

I draw myself up into a sitting position. My bedroom is full of golden morning light.

With a swift motion, I fling my legs out and step onto the ground. It springs beneath my feet. My wires click into motion, propelling me forward. I head out into the hallway, passing Ariel on my way there. We are both on our way for the morning salutations. My favorite part of the day.

We stroll out through the front door and step onto the sunny front lawn. Looking left and right, we see the other houses on either side of us, and the people walking out of them. The others follow the same movement. We all, at the exact same second, position ourselves at the edge of our yards and lift our arms up toward the sky.

We all open our mouths.

I cry out the words, *"ALL HAIL HXT AND ITS INFLUENCERS. ALL HAIL THE CEO. ALL HAIL THE COMPLACENCY TECHNOLOGY THAT MAKES US LOYAL FOREVER."*

One by one, everyone else lifts up their voice with the same greeting, and the collective sound roars through the perfect, plastic air.

THE END

About the Author

Viola Tempest is a dystopian fantasy and paranormal romance author who yearns to expose the truth of those in the modern world: the good, the bad, and the ugly. Her inspiration primarily stems from life experiences, those who annoy her, ex-boyfriends, and the crazy dreams that pop into her head every once in a while.

Stalk her below!

Website:
https://www.violatempest.com/

Facebook Page:
https://www.facebook.com/authorviolatempest

Instagram:
https://www.instagram.com/author_violatempest/

Goodreads:
https://www.goodreads.com/author/show/21693342.Viola_Tempest

BookBub:
https://www.bookbub.com/authors/viola-tempest